Chasing Kate

An American Dream Love Story

Book One

by

Josephine Parker

Editing by Chameleon
Cover Design by S.G. Hawkins

For Teri

Acknowledgment

Theodore Roosevelt once said, *"The credit belongs to the man who is actually in the arena, whose face is marred by dust, and sweat, and blood; who strives valiantly; who errs, who comes short again and again, because there is no effort without error and shortcoming; but who does actually strive to do the deeds; who knows great enthusiasms, the great devotions; who spends himself in a worthy cause; who at the best, knows in the end the triumph of high achievement, and who, at the worst, if he fails, at least fails while daring greatly."*

I scooted into the arena with a healthy nudge from an amazing group of friends, family, and beta readers, all of whom supported me along the way. My parents told me I could do anything and be anyone. My sister believed in my talent. My friends were there to listen when I cried, and cheer when I smiled. They all said, "Keep going." A greater fortune I could not imagine.

In particular, I'd like to thank Marilynn, Milt, Teri, Laurie H., Beth B., Melissa W., and Lauri O. You are the people most special to me in this world. Thank you for believing in me.

I would also like to thank Chameleon for her excellent editing, her guidance, and sharing her wealth of information. And S.G. Hawkins Graphic Design for tirelessly working to create the covers I envisioned.

Table of Contents

Chapter 1: Kate

Kate gripped the steering wheel tight as she leaned forward and peered through the dusty windshield of her rental car. The road she drove along rose and fell away in intervals, and each time she reached the crest of a new hill, she would sit up in her seat, only to sink back again in disappointment. There was not a building in sight.

As another row of spring-green fields curved away into the distance, she glared down at her GPS. The little red car crawled across the empty abyss of the screen, going nowhere. She flicked it with her finger and turned off the volume. If she heard it say, 'recalculating, recalculating', one more time, she'd throw it out the window.

Instead, she listened to the tires hum rhythmically on the pavement and tried to relax her grip.

Kate believed in second chances, but it would be hard to claim hers if she couldn't find it. She slapped her visor down and sat up higher in her seat to avoid the glare of sunlight cutting through some distant woods. She glanced down at her cell phone. Two bars. "Finally," she muttered. She put both hands on the steering wheel, turned on her blinker, and pulled slowly over to the side of the road.

She secured her Bluetooth headset onto her ear, then hit dial. As the phone began to ring, she glanced at the visor mirror and scowled at herself. Her normally wavy hair had mutated into Medusa-like dark coils that sprung from her head in all directions. *Damn Oklahoma air,* she thought. One more reason to finish this job and get home to Boston.

She rolled her eyes in exasperation as she tried to tame the tendrils back into place. As soon as she tucked one curl in, another sprung out. She looked at her pale blue eyes in the mirror and gave up. The best she could do was pin it back and hope it held.

"Hey, Pipes. You there?" Lindsey's voice came through the earpiece.

Kate exhaled. "You picked up."

"Duh. I've tried you like five times. Voice mail," Lindsey said. "Where are you?"

"No idea, but I must be close. My GPS thinks I'm off road." She looked around. "But I am on a road. A road with a whole lot of nothing around it."

Kate opened her car door and swung her legs out to give them a little shake, then got out of the car and stood on a crunchy patch of gravel as she looked around.

"How is it?" Lindsey asked. "Pretty?"

"Dusty," Kate said, peering into the distance. She watched two hawks circle around a nearby field and shivered. "Give me the city any day," Kate said. "What did you find on KinCo?"

"Right, business." Lindsey said. Kate could hear Lindsey's fingers tapping on her keyboard and imagined her at home in her basement bathed in the blue lights of her computer screens. "KinCo is family owned, founded in 1936. Get this, Pipes, they manufacture all kinds of stuff. I mean, everything from tissue to tires. Huge product line."

"Problems?"

"Weirdly, no," Lindsey answered. "At least, not so far. I'm still digging. They have a great brand, good name recognition, and, like, no catastrophes. Crazy, right?"

"Hmm," Kate murmured, wondering why she got the call late last night. "I guess we'll find out soon enough. Something must be up."

"Well, it's a new adventure, at least," Lindsey

said.

Kate was grateful she still had Lindsey by her side. "Thanks again for jumping on this at such a late hour. After everything…"

Lindsey's fingers paused on her keyboard. "Yeah," she said. "Anything for you, Pipes."

Last night, Kate was packing boxes in her office, ready to turn off the lights for good. It's hard to stay open as a Reputation Manager when no one wants you to manage their reputation. She knew she was good at what she did, but she made the mistake of crossing the wrong person, quitting her last job, and going out on her own. She thought with hard work and talent she could achieve her American Dream. She was wrong. She was getting used to that idea when the phone rang. It was the assistant to Cal Kincaid, President of KinCo, asking her to fly out as soon as possible. That was all the info Kate had, but it was enough to give her hope that all was not lost. She called Lindsey to do some meeting prep, then got on the first flight out.

"Good job, Lindz," Kate said. "Keep me posted on what else you find."

"I will," Lindsey assured her, then she paused. "This is a big deal," she finally said.

Kate nodded. "I know."

"You have to land this job."

Kate put her hands on her hips and inhaled. "I know," she said in a rush as she exhaled. She felt pressure building at the base of her neck. Her voice had trembled just a bit. No one else but Lindsey would have even heard it. Kate heard Lindsey's hands pause on the keyboard.

"Do you need a fluff?" Lindsey asked quietly.

Kate laughed. "God yes," she said, and leaned back against the car with a smile.

"Okay." Lindsey began. "You listen to me, Kate Piper. You are amazing, and you are going to get this job," she said. "You are brilliant and beautiful, and any smart company would want to hire you. If they don't, they're not smart, and we don't work for dumb people, do we?"

"No."

"No," Lindsey said, "that's right. And these must be smart people because they have built a huge, successful company, and they were smart enough to call you. So, you are going to march right in there and let them see how amazing you are with your wicked spidey-sense and your get-things-done attitude." Lindsey took a breath, then said, "You're Kate Freaking Piper. And they don't know who they're messing with, right?"

"Right."

"Right," she said. "Now, who are you?"

"Kate Piper, dammit."

"That's right! Shoulders back, take a big, deep breath, give yourself a little stretch, Kate Piper. You are going to kill this."

Kate raised her hands over her head and

breathed deeply. She felt the fluff and the sunshine build her confidence, but as she spread her arms wide, she felt the top button on her blouse pop off and roll away. "Shit!" Her arms fell back to her side as she eyed the ground around her.

"What happened?"

"I lost one of my buttons," Kate said as she glanced at the gap the missing button had opened up. She could see the deep crevice between her breasts, and the lacy curve of each side of her bra. She should have known this would happen when she dug this blouse out of the back of the closet, wrinkled and smashed into a corner. She tried to freshen it up with a dryer sheet and some spray, but she hadn't thought to see if it still fit well. Rookie mistake. Two years ago, when she was on top of her game, this never would have happened. She didn't even remember to pack a sewing kit.

"I can't go in there like this," she said as she tried to pull the shirt back together. "Like, hello there, I'm Kate Piper, Reputation Manager, please ignore my tits and hire me. I promise you, nothing this embarrassing will ever happen to you."

She groaned, then got down on her knees and swept under the car with her arm. That's when she saw the pickup truck idling behind her. "Whoa," she said, sitting back on her heels. "Wait a minute."

"Find it?" Lindsey said into Kate's ear.

"There's some guy behind me in a truck." Kate said as she raised her hand to shade her eyes.

"Holy crap," Lindsey said. "You're all by yourself out there. What's he doing?"

"Staring."

"Holy crap. What is he, some kind of drifter?"

"Dunno," Kate said. "Might be two guys. No. Guy and a dog. He's getting out."

"Holy crap. Should I call the police?"

"Shhh, hold on."

Kate watched as the man got out of his truck and shut the door, then crossed his arms without a word, watching her.

"What's happening?" Lindsey asked.

"Hold on," Kate whispered.

A small gust of wind swirled around Kate as she and the man surveyed each other silently. Kate glanced down through her open car door wondering what she might be able to make into a weapon. Maybe there was still time to jump in and drive away. The man uncrossed his arms and began to walk toward her.

Kate widened her stance and stood as tall as she could. She mustered her toughest Boston voice and called out, "Stop right there."

The man stopped.

Kate tried to get a better look at him. "Can I help you with something?" She barked.

The man tilted his head and looked at her from beneath the rim of his baseball hat. Wow, he was tall. And solid. Kate watched as he bent slightly at the waist and looked past her into her car.

Kate sucked in her breath. From there, he could see she was alone. He eyed her warily, then gave a little shake of his head. He gestured vaguely in her direction. "Looks like you're the one that could use the help," he called out.

Kate swallowed. "Um—yes. I'm looking for KinCo, do you—" As she clutched the two sides of her blouse together, the man turned away silently and walked back to his truck.

"He went back to his truck," Kate whispered to Lindsey.

"What's he doing?"

"It looks like…wait," she said. "He's gotten out a tool box and taken something out of it. He's walking back."

"Oh my God," Lindsey said. "Is it an axe? If it's an axe, I'm calling the police."

Kate reached out to brace herself against the side of the car. She felt her heart racing. "No, you're not," she said. "Hold on."

The man sauntered back to Kate, then stopped, eyeing her from about five feet away. He wore a plaid shirt and a boyish baseball cap, from beneath which Kate could see two scowling, light colored eyes, and a clenched jaw covered with stubble. It seemed like he was deciding something. Apparently satisfied, he continued to walk toward her. He stretched out a grease-stained hand. "Here you go," he said, glancing down at her busted-open shirt.

Kate looked down. He held a safety pin in his hand. She flushed and crossed her arms." Right," she said. "Oops." She stepped toward him and untangled one arm to reach out for the pin. As she did, a rush of warm air surrounded her. She chalked it up to Oklahoma heat, but then their eyes locked. His were a mossy green with a burst of gold flecks around the center. Kate felt something shift deep inside her. As he handed her the safety pin, he leaned forward to speak softly in her ear. "KinCo is about two miles straight down the road. You can't miss it." He leaned back and gave her a smile. "You have a nice day, now." Without another word, he got in his truck and left.

Kate was dazed. She plucked at her collar to try to get some air to her skin. She watched as the truck pulled away in a plume of dust, then got back in her car and blasted the air. It was a moment before she realized Lindsey was talking in her ear.

"What happened, Kate? What's happening?"

Kate felt a lazy smile pull at her lips. "Good Lord, they make them hot out here." It was all she could say in response.

"Who? The drifter?"

"Yeah," she said, smiling, "hot drifter."

"Kate! Focus, Kate," Lindsey said. "Keep your eye on the balls. Ball! You're going to be late."

Kate felt her mind sink back on track like a gear popping into place. "Right," she said, starting the engine. She chastised herself for getting distracted so close to a meeting that could save her company.

"You're right," Kate said, pulling forward into the sun. "I'm on it. It's a beautiful day for redemption."

Chapter 2: Chase

It was a warm Oklahoma morning when Chase Kincaid pulled up to his bungalow in a swhirl of dust and gravel. He'd made good time, as always, and jumped out of his truck like a schoolboy. He turned back to see his dog, Fitz, staring up at him from the passenger seat with wet, black eyes, his enormous tail thumping loudly against the seat. "Come on, boy," Chase said with a sweep of his arm. Fitz bounded across the seat and landed on the ground below. He circled around Chase twice then ambled over to the lawn to sniff the hedges and bark a squirrel up a tree before following Chase inside.

It had been cool and quiet this morning when Chase had made his daily trip to check out the trucks pulling in and out of the factory. He liked to come just before shift change, when sparkling stars still dangled above, and the sky began to bloom in the pastel light. He could taste last night's dew evaporating in the air as the KinCo trucks rumbled out of the factory gates full of deliveries. He still had the same rush of excitement seeing them drive off as he did when he was a kid and his grandpa took him to see the factory for the first time.

"Stand back now, Chase, and don't touch anything," he'd said. "These are working men, here to do a job. Always respect that."

Chase immediately loved the elegant rush and click of the machinery, and the orchestration of bodies on the line and in the bays. As a kid, Chase felt the magic in all the disparate parts coming together, building towards something new and better. He felt a surge in his belly thinking about it. Six more weeks and the company would be his.

Fitz meandered over to the kitchen and gave a happy whine as Chase filled his water and food bowls. Chase bent down and gave Fitz a hearty rub around the ears. "Who's a good boy?" he asked.

Fitz perked up his ears.

"You, that's right."

Fitz collapsed onto his side and exposed his belly in response.

"Okay, killer." Chase rubbed his belly. "You

keep a good eye on the house today. I'll see you when I get home." Fitz sprang up and spread his big jowly mouth into a smile. Chase was certain Fitz would salute him if he could. "Good boy," he said again, then walked towards the shower, peeling his clothes off on the way.

Chase turned the water on full force and stepped in, taking a moment to let the hot water stream down his neck and back. He couldn't put his finger on it, but he felt like something bad was coming, but how could it? Everything was going according to plan. He smiled at himself and his nerves. He was damn well not going to waste another day brooding. This was a happy time. His parents were finally going to retire, and Aunt Peggy would get to monetize the company, just like she'd been pushing to do for years. He ran through the same mental checklist he ran through several times a day, then shook his head and let the warm water rush over him.

Some strange stuff had been happening lately, but he thought maybe the high expectations were making him paranoid. He had to stop trolling around the back roads trying to find more strange cars hanging around, checking out the KinCo trucks coming and going. At least one of those cars had held a crazy person this week, so now he tried to keep his distance. Until today, at least.

Chase lathered himself and wondered who that woman on the side of the road was this morning. Armies of attorneys and accountants had been coming and going in the past few weeks. Seeing a new face was nothing new, but another strange car idling on the side of the road made him nervous. As he hung back to check it out, he was surprised to see a woman emerge. And even from that distance, he could see she was an attractive woman. He smiled. That woman could wear a skirt and a pair of heels. And that dark hair blowing in the wind. He felt like a voyeur, standing back and watching her stretch, then bend over as she searched the ground for something. He'd felt no shame as he zoned in on those curves. And he was even more pleasantly surprised when he got closer. Whoever she was, she was gorgeous.

He should make the rounds after his meeting with Big Cal and keep an eye out for her. He had a strict no-fraternizing policy when it came to KinCo employees, which basically meant everyone in town, but maybe this girl was a contract worker. In and out. No harm there, right? A romp in the sack with a beautiful woman would definitely help bring down his anxiety level—especially with one who would be leaving shortly thereafter.

He knew she was beautiful from his truck, but what he wasn't expecting was the pull he felt when he got closer. That attitude of hers. And that adorable accent. She was trying to be tough, and he didn't blame her, being on the road by herself. The attitude was kind of hot. He was sure that, later, when they really met and she found out who he was, she'd feel bad about that. And she would be looking to feel better. And he would be there, happy to help her feel better. He remembered those eyes, that neck, and that smart mouth just begging to be kissed. And he would yank open that busted shirt and suck on those soft tits as he pushed her down on the hood of the car. She would be yanking on his hair as she begged him not to stop, and he wouldn't, he wouldn't stop until, until…

A loud groan escaped Chase as he finished off into the warm stream of the shower. He had to lean against the tile for a few minutes to catch his breath. He laughed out loud. No harm in a little imagination, he told himself. It was times like these he was glad he lived alone so no one could hear him. Well, Fitz could hear him, but Fitz was used to it.

Six more weeks, he told himself as he shaved and got dressed. He took one last look in the mirror before he headed out the door. *It's good to be me,* he thought.

Chapter 3: Kate

A woman with a tight bun met Kate at the security office. She introduced herself curtly as, "Constance, Assistant to the President", affixed VISITOR credentials to Kate's chest, then turned with a straight back and walked toward a bank of elevators. Kate followed. As the doors closed, Kate flipped over her wrist and checked her watch. Ten minutes late. She silently cursed the woman for making her wait so long, shooting her a sideways glance. Maybe her bun was so tight it inhibited her motor skills.

As the doors to the executive floor opened, Kate had the urge to dart out in front, but she didn't know where she was going. Instead, she gave the woman a nod and a smile, then followed her out and down the hall.

Kate was ushered into a brightly lit waiting area just outside the President's office. As soon as her escort turned away, Kate scrambled around, trying to find any information she could on KinCo. Just as she found a product brochure, she heard a man yelling.

"Balls! Balls, dammit!"

Kate watched as Constance turned toward the office with an audible sigh.

"Constance! Get your tail in here," the yelling continued.

Constance pushed herself up from her desk and stomped through the open office door.

Kate bent sideways and peeked through the window. A white-haired man was holding a computer mouse in his hand and looking in despair at the screen. He raised the mouse up, then slammed it on the desk, slid it around, then looked to the screen hopefully.

He frowned. He picked up the mouse and slammed it on the desk again with a pop. Kate watched as Constance reached out to take the mouse away.

"No," she said. "*No,* Cal. That won't work." She slapped the back of his hand like a schoolteacher and yanked the mouse from him. She reached over the desk and pulled the keyboard toward her, pecking something quickly on the keys.

"I sent it to myself," she said. "I'll do it. Jeez."

The man looked up and caught Kate spying. She began to lean back but he shot her a sheepish grin. "Busted," he said. "I guess you can come on in, Ms. Piper."

Kate nodded and stood, straightening her skirt. As she gathered her things, Constance walked back out to her desk. On the way, she gave Kate a little wink and a smile.

Dorothy, I don't think we're in Kansas anymore, Kate thought to herself. *I am a long way from Boston.*

She walked into the office and extended a hand. "Mr. Kincaid?" she asked with a smile. "Hello, I'm Kate Piper."

Cal Kincaid stood to greet her, his enormous shoulders raised in a shrug. "Ms. Piper, I do apologize. You caught me with my pants down. I never could figure out those mice."

"Mouse!" shouted Constance from the lobby.

"Right," said Cal. "Never could get the hang of it. I'll be happy if I never have to see one of those things again. Anyway," he said, gesturing towards a chair, "Please, sit down."

Kate looked around the office, surprised by how different it was from the rest of the KinCo building. She was transported back thirty years. The walls were wood paneling, covered with dozens of mostly black and white photos. As she sat, her chair sighed with the pleasure of worn, soft leather. Even Cal Kincaid looked like a man from a bygone era. He wore boots with his suit, and his jacket sported elbow patches and shoulder epaulets. He wore no tie, just an open plaid shirt that revealed tufts of white hair that matched the perfectly pomaded shock of white hair that covered his head.

Cal hitched up one side of his belt, then the other. He did not sit. Instead, he rested the tips of his fingers tentatively on the edge of his desk.

"This is a tricky time for KinCo, Ms. Piper," he said. "I expect you've guessed that much or you wouldn't be here." He began to pace back and forth in the space between his desk and the massive bookshelf behind it when Kate heard a tiny click of the door opening. She turned to see Constance stick her head in.

"Here you go, Cal" she said as she handed him a stack of papers.

"Very good, Connie, thank you."

Kate watched Constance close the office door gingerly as she left. Through the glass windows, she could see three employees waiting for Constance at her desk. She chatted with them briefly, then handed each of them a small box of Tupperware she pulled from a giant bag. Kate turned back before she was caught staring.

Cal took the stack of papers behind his desk. By Kate's estimation, the desk was at least eighty years old and must weigh four hundred pounds. Its massive corners were carved like wooden rope, which seemed to draw up its muscle against the cords that trailed from Cal's computer and spilled over the edge. The keyboard and monitor were tucked as far to one side of the desk as possible.

Cal sat down, moving aside stacks of paper held together by binder clips and covered in sticky notes.

"Ms. Piper, I feel a little funny asking you this," Cal said with a little laugh, "but I'm sure you're used to it in your business." He pointed to the stack of papers Constance had carried in. "I have here, to my thinking, a ridiculously thick Non-Disclosure Agreement." He pushed the papers towards Kate. "If you would be so kind as to sign it. After your thorough examination, of course." He gave Kate a smile. "Thanks to Connie, you'll see it's marked where you need to sign and initial."

Kate took the papers and flipped through them. The NDA was standard, although not necessary. She would never disclose any information about a client, current or former. She took the papers with a smile. "Happy to sign, Mr. Kincaid," she said, her pen in hand.

"Cal, if it's okay with you, Ms. Piper. Big Cal, if we become friends, which I hope we do."

"Alright, Cal. Then I'm Kate, if that's okay with you."

They smiled at each other and Kate waited for

him to speak.

"What do you know about KinCo, Kate?"

Kate bristled. She preferred to have more information than anyone else in the room so she could pull from that information like a carpenter with a toolbox. Sitting in front of Cal, she felt like she needed a hammer and all she had was a tie-twist. She was glad Lindsey was able to find some basic info in the few hours they had to prepare.

"KinCo was founded in the 1930s and is a manufacturer of various goods," Kate said. "It is privately held and run. You seem to have a loyal customer base and very little scandal. In fact, in a basic search, very little can be found about your company. Your reputation seems in very good shape."

Kate flattened her hands, leaned forward just a bit and lowered her voice, "You must have concerns that's about to change, however," she said, "or I wouldn't be here."

Cal tapped his fingers on the table twice, then stood. "May I show you something, Kate?" He walked around the desk to the far wall which was covered with black and white photos. Kate stood and joined him.

"I grew up in this company, in this town." Cal began, pointing at a grainy picture of a young boy standing in front of a silo painted with the KinCo logo. "I've never known anything else, and never wanted to." He pointed to another photo. "My mother and father started KinCo during The Great Depression. They weren't looking to build a company, they just wanted to help their neighbors. Back then, this town was almost all farmers, but after the Depression hit, most trucks stopped running and folks couldn't sell their crops, or buy anything else they needed." Cal reached out to touch a photo of a woman standing on a porch in a simple smock, waving at the camera with a stern but honest smile. "My mom took every penny she had to build a local mill. A place neighbors could come with their corn or grain and grind it down to flour. Nobody had any money, so she took food in exchange. Soon, she found people needed certain things and had other things to barter, so her mill turned into a little store for the community.

Cal pointed at another photo. "If a thing was needed, and nobody had it, why, my mom just figured out how to make it. That's how KinCo started. Just a neighborhood store that gave folks what they needed. After my parents were gone, I took over. I spent the first twenty years just hoping I didn't shit the bed, if you'll excuse my language."

Kate nodded.

"Then, by what I can only consider grace from above, I met my wife, Rosemary." Cal showed her a photo of a woman in a lab coat and protective glasses holding up a beaker for the camera. "We built KinCo into a national brand with just a few more products." He winked.

After a moment, he looked back at the array of photos. "This company, these people, are—" he began, placing his palm on the wall, "have been our whole life. We've been happy here, have made lifelong friends and raised our son. I have been a very lucky man."

Kate looked up to see Cal's eyes shining. "I'm a big softy," he said. "Don't tell anybody."

"Your secret's safe with me," Kate said.

Cal nodded, then put his thumbs through his belt loops and his weight back on his heels. "Things change, though. I know that." He ushered Kate back to sit down.

As Kate sat, she felt the familiar crackle in the air that only came before someone divulged the most personal of information. She waited silently.

"Ms. Piper—" Cal said before correcting himself. "Kate, the time has come for me to retire and pass the torch. My Rose had to leave the company last year. Her arthritis got too bad. Now, I just want to spend time with her, maybe travel." He took a breath. "Rose wants to take one of those European River Cruises, you know. Doesn't matter to me what we do. I just want to see her smile."

"I understand," said Kate.

"My sister, Peggy, our CFO, has been pushing us for some time to make a significant change, and my retirement seems like a good time to make it happen. My son, Chase, agrees with her." Cal paused, his brows drawing together. "They want to take KinCo public."

Kate felt her fingers tighten against her thighs. She never moved her eyes from Cal Kincaid as her heart quickened in her chest.

He continued. "We have a good thing here, and going public is risky, but it also brings advantages that we can't get otherwise."

Kate nodded.

"To be honest, this whole IPO business makes me feel undressed. Like I'm standing here in only my socks. It's a whole new world, I guess. Gone are the days when having the best product was enough. Now we have to assure the public we have the best leadership. Especially during this transition," he said. "This is where you come in, Kate. A good friend of mine suggested I call you."

Kate's eyes widened. She thought she didn't have an ally left in the world. Who would have recommended her?

Cal continued. "Basically, I need you to cover my hind-end. Protect our reputation through the launch, and make sure nothing tanks us. The Public, God help us, must have total faith in our ability to continue growing." He shook his head. "This thing is happening. My one requirement—and this is non-negotiable, is that the company still be controlled and run by family.

We can only do that if the family reputation remains intact."

"I see," said Kate.

"The way Peggy has this thing set up, the majority of shares will stay with family. Chase will be made CEO."

"What is his function now?"

"Chief Operating Officer. I'm President only for this final stretch. Then Chase will run the whole enchilada."

Kate's stomach flipped. This wasn't just some back-corner, two-day job. Pulling into the KinCo parking lot this morning, she expected someone to ask her to fix the company's social media presence or try to remove some negative reviews. She hoped to get a week of work and pay her much overdo office rent. But this was different. This job could save her. If she could say she was part of a successful IPO launch, she would definitely get more work, even if there was still one evil bitch bent on her destruction. Kate gripped the arms of her chair. She didn't know how this happened, but she told herself that maybe things really do work out if you do the right thing, just like her mother always said.

"Today, you will meet Peggy, Chase, and the rest of the team. We have a corporate house for you to stay in during your time here." He paused. "I hope that's okay? I hope you don't have another job that will take you away in the next few weeks. I'd feel more comfortable if you were close by."

Hell, yes! She thought, but reigned herself in. "Of course, Cal, whatever you need," she said. "I do have one key employee I'd like to bring in remotely as support. I assume you'll also need an NDA from her?"

"Yes, we'll email that to you for her signature."

"You'll have it back by the end of the day."

"Now, full disclosure." He swept some invisible dust off the corner of the desk. "I made the decision to bring you in last night, and our time line being what it is, did not allow me the opportunity to loop in Peggy and Chase."

"I see."

"Peggy might bristle a bit." He lowered his voice. "That woman can get her underpants bunched up faster than anyone I've ever known, but she'll get on board. I'll talk to her."

"And your son?"

"He's a gem." Cal beamed. "He runs most of the company already. Hell, he'll probably do a better job than I ever did. However, I will admit, he does have a general distrust of all things PR."

"Oh?" Kate said. "Why is that?"

"He'll explain, I'm sure," Cal said. "I will tell you that this IPO is the most important thing in the world to Chase. There's no way he'd endanger it. Oh–" Cal said, glancing out his office window into the hall, "here he is now."

Kate turned and looked out the glass. There was a tall man in a suit talking to Constance. She handed him a piece of Tupperware, followed by a hug. He turned and walked toward Cal's office, then stopped when he saw Kate inside. A strange look washed over his face.

"Chase, this is Kate Piper," Cal said as the door pushed open.

Kate stood.

"Well, hello there, Ms. Piper," Chase said. "I see you found your way here."

Kate froze. Tall, light eyes. She tried to imagine this slick, perfect businessman in a baseball cap, face covered with stubble. Could this be the hot drifter from this morning? *Oh my God,* she thought, *it is him.*

She brought her hand to the safety pin holding her blouse together.

"Um, yes," she said. "Thanks again for the directions."

Chase turned to Cal, "On the way from the shop, I saw Ms. Piper on the road trying to find her way."

Cal began to apologize for not sending a car, and grumbled how nobody could ever find them, but Kate could barely hear him. She was locked in a gaze with Chase that muted everything else. The room began to buzz. She felt some thought floating just out of reach, but she couldn't put her hands on it.

"Kate is here to help us for the next few weeks," Cal said.

"Is that right?" Chase said, looking pleased.

"Kate's come from Boston," Cal continued. "She's a Reputation Manager."

Chase tore his gaze from Kate and looked at Cal, dumbfounded. "A What?"

"Now, Son, she's not here to slap you around. She's just here to manage our image going into the launch. Makes sense, right?"

Chase looked at him flatly. "Hell, no," he said.

Kate began to speak, but Cal stood, silencing her. "Kate, would you excuse us, please. I think my son would like to have a word in private."

Kate gathered her things and stepped out. As she glanced back into the office she saw Chase staring at her, his light eyes peering at her with suspicion. Yup, Kate thought, this is definitely the hot drifter with his distrusting face and clenched muscles. She pulled out her phone and texted Lindsey. "Get me as much as you can on Chase Kincaid, COO."

Kate turned back towards the office to see Cal talking to Chase. He put his hand on Chase's shoulder and gave it a little squeeze. Chase dropped his head and put his hand on the desk. Kate could swear she saw a slight smile then a shake of his head as if he were admonishing himself. Then he stood and shoved both fists down into his pockets and nodded at Cal. They finally shook hands and walked toward the office door.

Kate straightened as they walked out. Cal turned to Kate. "We appreciate you flying out here and lending us your expertise on such short notice." He extended a hand to Kate. "Chase will be taking you to his office now, where the two of you can hammer out exactly what you need."

"Sure. No problem," Chase said in response, but Kate could feel his animosity building with each word. She wanted to shake him, slap him, or kiss him. Anything to remove the disdain from his face.

"Chase and I will work together, Cal. I'm sure I'll be able to explain what I do in a way that makes him feel more at ease." Kate tilted her head and gave him a half smile.

A successful IPO launch for KinCo would also re-launch her own career, and she wasn't going to be thwarted by one spoiled ego-maniac. As she followed Chase to his office, she resolved that she would keep him in check for the next month. He wouldn't be easy, but she'd worked with tougher clients than this. Hell, she could floss her teeth with this guy. Now, if she could just manage to control herself…

Chapter 4: Chase

Chase took giant strides to stay ahead of Kate as they left Big Cal and walked through the glossy halls of KinCo in silence. He expected to hear the click of her heels scurrying to keep up, but instead, Kate hung back as if she was some dignitary he was escorting on a company tour. The faster he walked, the slower Kate followed. He felt the blood rising up past his collar and into his face.

Chase Kincaid did not need a Reputation Manager. The idea was ridiculous.

As he entered his office, he smoothed down his tie and gathered his thoughts. This day was not going the way he had hoped.

When Kate caught up, he motioned for her to

take the chair opposite his desk. She set her notebook on his desk, then sat easily, sweeping one perfect leg over the other and waited. A long moment passed as Chase looked across at Kate in exasperation, although he hoped it didn't show. He silently considered how to break her down. To put her in a tiny little package he could put the lid on and keep in the corner until this month was over.

Chase waited for her to give in and say something. Instead, she looked at him patiently with her liquid blue eyes. He couldn't believe he was letting this woman beat him at his own game. If he wasn't careful, she would end up getting everything she wanted from him. He wasn't sure yet what that was, but Kate was a Reputation Manager, and to him, that was the same as Professional Manipulator, so he knew it wouldn't be good. He imagined himself in a clown costume with shackles and felt his blood pressure rise. He'd better change tactics and get the upper hand before she had him trailing out of here like a trained puppy.

He cleared his throat.

"Ms. Piper," he began, "I'm sure you're tired after your adventure filled ride from the airport, so let's cut this short. How about you tell me what you need so I can get on with my day."

Chase couldn't be sure, but he thought he saw the trace of a smile pass by Kate's lips.

"I'm here to help you," she said, then added, "I can do that if you'll let me."

"That's sure nice of you, Ms. Piper. Thing is, I don't need help."

"Everybody needs help."

He smiled and gave her his best *Oh Shucks* Oklahoma grin and ran his hands through his hair. "Well, I'm sure a lot of people do, Ms. Piper, and I'm sure you've seen a bunch." He leaned forward. "I can only imagine the kind of shit you've shoveled."

He watched her shift in her chair and continued. "Problem for you is, there's nothing going on here that would require your type of service."

"My type of service?" Kate asked. "What is that, exactly?"

Chase felt his jaw tighten. "My dirty laundry is not hanging outside my window for everybody to see. I've gone to great lengths to make sure I'm insulated." Chase felt a stab in his heart as he admitted this. If Kate only knew how isolated he had made himself to protect his reputation she would pity him. "I don't do drugs, I don't send pictures of my genitals over social media. I don't take secret trips to Bangkok. There has never been a sexual harassment suit at KinCo, on the books or off. So there are no skeletons that you need to dust off and put a pretty bow on." He leaned back as if he had handily won the discussion. "If you would like me to have you set up at a corner desk where you can Google me all day for a month, I'd be happy to do that for you, although I'm sure that would be boring for someone like you."

Kate cocked her head and smiled. "I'm sure you have done an excellent job managing your reputation..." She tapped her pen on her leg and looked around. "Until now. Even though your philosophy might be a little short sighted."

"Are you trying to insult me?"

"You make bumpers here, don't you?" Kate asked.

Chase leaned back, unsure where she was going. "Bumpers? For cars? Yes, we do."

"And a lot of time and engineering goes into those bumpers, I'm sure."

"Right..."

"And the bumper has to be strong and protect the vehicle, no matter the risk or speed?"

"Right..."

"But you have a special kind of bumper that has an extra layer of resistance, right?"

Chase nodded.

"And this bumper is meant just as extra protection, right? All the engineering and heavy lifting is done by the car itself. The bumper just protects all the other work that's gone into the body of the car." She leaned forward and placed her palms on his desk. "Think of me as your bumper."

As Chase let out a tiny laugh, he felt his blood-pressure drop back to a normal level. "You want to be my bumper."

"I do."

"That's interesting."

"Let me explain."

"Please, do."

Kate leaned back and crossed her legs. "You do a lot of work here. You create and manufacture a myriad of products successfully. You are a major employer. It's impressive. But all this work," she motioned with her hand, "all of it is at risk. All your work could be destroyed if this launch goes badly. You can control a lot of it, true. But a dent in your reputation is like a juggernaut that can fly out of control and destroy you. I'm sure you understand how important your reputation is to this launch."

Kate paused as she watched his eyebrows draw together, then continued. "I'm sure you remember the launch of a very famous social media company—you might not participate in social media yourself, but this launch was big. You couldn't have missed it."

"Right…"

"Well, that CEO waltzed into a meeting with his investors wearing a hoodie and his valuation tanked. They didn't trust his commitment because of his wardrobe. Something as simple as a hoodie can hurt your launch." Kate took a beat to meet his gaze. "I can see already how important this is to you. You manage a myriad of quickly moving parts. Let me look out for the other things that might endanger the launch–things that you might not see coming."

Chase felt the air go out of him. "I'm listening," he said.

"Now more than ever, you need a barrier. Think of me as an extra layer of protection that covers all your hard work." She smiled.

"Okay," Chase said, "I'll play along. How do you do that?"

"Reputation Management is an art. Instead of handling a crisis once it's already started, my job is to anticipate problems and cut them off before they can grow and hurt you or your company. I do this by taking in all the information I can about you, your goals, any existing problems, and any potential enemies. I deduce likely scenarios. If there is any rumor, I change the narrative. If you have enemies, I anticipate and diffuse their next move. In other words, if anyone wants to hit you, I deflect them." Kate put both of her hands flat on the desk and looked Chase in the eye. Her voice sank soft and low. "That's what makes me a good bumper."

Kate leaned back with an ease and power Chase had not seen before. He believed her. He felt a warm sensation run through his chest as he took her in, so calm and sure. He wanted to climb over the desk and curl up in her lap. This was a whole new experience for him. "Alright," he said, "I can't believe I'm going to say this, but what do you need from me?"

Kate grinned. "I need to interview you and your team. I need access to all your social media and PR materials. I'd like to get started right away if—"

Kate was interrupted by a buzz on his phone and a voice breaking in. "Chase, Peggy is here to see you."

Chase exhaled and rubbed his brow. "Okay, let her in."

The door burst open and a tall, thin woman strode in. "Cal told me but I couldn't believe it," she said, casting her eyes down to Kate. "I had to see it for myself. Reputation Manger, huh? My God, what will people start calling themselves tomorrow? Likability Monitor? Or, how about Confidence Enhancer? Yeah," she practically spat, "some people will fall for anything if you let 'em."

Chase stood and stared at his aunt. "Peggy, let's not rush to judgment."

Kate stood and extended her hand. "Hello, Ms. Kincaid. Kate Piper."

Peggy hesitated, then offered a limp hand. "I'm not used to being second guessed," Peggy said, "and frankly, I have not wrapped my head around just what you're doing here." She raised her shoulders as if in disbelief. "More evidence of my brother's aging mind."

"Aunt Peggy," Chase interrupted, "hear Kate out. After listening to her, I have to say, I don't see any harm in working with her."

Peggy snickered. "I'm sure you're just chomping at the bit to work with her, Chase." Peggy shook her head, looking Kate up and down. "Men," she added dismissively.

Kate smiled. "I think I have what I need to get started," she said as she grabbed her bag. She paused at the door and turned to Chase. "Mr. Kincaid, we can pick this up again tomorrow."

Chase stood, dumbfounded, as he watched her depart. Twenty minutes ago he couldn't wait to get rid of this woman and now he wanted to run after her and ask her to come back. She had an unnerving effect on him. He must have had this written all over his face because Peggy snapped her fingers and said, "Hey, snap out of it, Chase. Keep it in your pants. We have a lot on the line here."

Chase shook his head. Peggy was right. Of all the times in his life to get distracted by a woman, this was the worst. The thought of all the people depending on him rushed into his mind. She could do her work and he would do his, but if he couldn't control how he felt about her, he'd better keep his distance.

Chapter 5: Kate

Kate slept better than she had in months. She stretched her limbs out beneath the thick, fluffy comforter and slowly opened her eyes. Morning sunlight was pouring through slats in the windows, bathing the room in a soft yellow light. There was a slight hum coming from outside. Kate blinked a few times, then bolted upright. It took her a minute to realize where she was. She wasn't in Boston. She was inside a bungalow on the KinCo corporate housing compound.

Kate leapt out of bed and ran to the window. How late had she slept? She peered outside at the morning sun. Good. It wasn't too late. She could jump in the shower and hurry to KinCo headquarters and beat most everyone there. She would arrive later than she liked, but still early enough to be respectable.

Outside her window, she saw perfectly manicured lawns and sidewalks dotted with flower beds. The compound held about eight identical brick bungalows, as far as she could see, each linked to the other by a curving series of walkways. Last night, when she was about to leave KinCo, Constance had brought her a manila envelope filled with information about the company, her visitor ID, a parking pass, and a smaller envelope which held a key to this house. The key was attached to an information sheet with directions to the house, how to order groceries, and a copy of their No Smoking policy.

"I assumed I'd be staying in a hotel," Kate said to Constance as she pulled out the key.

"Oh no, honey. There are no hotels anywhere near here. Cal's parents built the bungalows in the thirties when housing was hard to find. Used to be all family, but now they like to keep a couple of houses empty for visitors."

"I see. That's nice."

"It is. Lovely place. Cal and Rosemary are next door, and Chase is across the way, so it makes everything real easy."

Kate peered out the window at the door directly across from hers. The blinds were drawn and there was no sign anyone was home. Kate wondered if Chase was in there. She shook her head as she remembered her reaction to meeting him in Cal's office. *Silly Kate,* she thought. *It's not like you've never been near an attractive man before. Super attractive. Crazy attractive. Get it together, Kate,* she scolded herself.

This was the most important job of her life, and she felt like a dribbling idiot in his office. Once they were alone behind closed doors, she could barely speak. She had to keep coaching herself silently to get her head in the game. Her mind swirled with words but nothing would come out. She sat there like a mute. She hoped he didn't notice. Thank goodness he spoke first and gave her time to get her thoughts in order.

After a good night's sleep, and a chance to wrap her arms around how much this job could mean to her future, Kate was ready to dig in. She was going to annihilate this job. She was going to crush it.

Kate pried the window blinds open a little wider and looked once more at Chase's bungalow across a perfect sea of green lawn. Only he stood between her and success. He wouldn't be easy to manage, but he could see reason, and that was a good start. She bit down on her lip. He was also easy to look at. Good lord, that man could wear a suit. And a pair of jeans. She wondered if he was in that bungalow right now wearing anything at all. She shook her head, disgusted with herself. She let the blinds snap shut and shuffled off to the kitchen to put on a pot of coffee and check her email.

Kate leaned against the kitchen counter and set up her laptop. She opened Wi-Fi settings and saw a network, but she didn't have the password. She reached for the manila envelope again and looked through the information. Drat. Nothing. She checked her phone. After updating Lindsey with all the sordid details of the day via text message, Lindsey flooded her email with various files on the comp, but reading them on her phone would be a nightmare. She ran to turn on the shower. If she hurried into headquarters she could use the Wi-Fi there. She called Lindsey as she stripped off her clothes.

"Hey, girl," Lindsey answered.

"Hey. Whatcha got? Besides mad skills, of course."

"Not as much as you'd think, really."

"Really?"

"Yeah. Mr. Chase Kincaid, AKA the Hot Drifter, doesn't seem to have many issues. He's almost squeaky clean."

"Huh. Well, I guess that makes things easier. Background?"

"Looks like Chase was raised out there in KinCo land, then, as a teenager, was sent off to prep school. He got a Bachelors in Business, and Masters in Business Economics. Ivy League, of course."

"Of course."

"Most of what I found percolated around that time and in the three or so years after he graduated."

"Like what?"

"The typical. Pictures on social media of him partying, hanging onto girls, stumbling out of nightclubs, the usual."

"Nothing crazy? That's good."

"Yeah, but about seven years ago he was highlighted in a national article on most eligible bachelors. And, by the way, holy crap that guy is hot!"

"He's a client," Kate said, mostly to remind herself.

"Sure, but that doesn't mean he can't be ogled online by me and any other girl with a pulse," Lindsey said. "His Internet presence shot up for a while. You know, Facebook posts of old pictures sprung up, lots of tweets. Rumors of romantic dalliances here and there. Then it looks like the KinCo racing team was involved in an accident. Chase was driving and some woman was hit on the raceway. After that, I couldn't find much."

"Hold up. KinCo has a racing team?"

"Had. Chase was the driver in several regional races, but it looks like the team was disbanded. Nothing recent."

"Okay, good. All we need is a 'fast-women, fast-cars' narrative to surface."

"Nope, I don't think so."

Kate gripped the counter. "Good," she said. "Hopefully, this will be smooth sailing. You got the NDA I sent you?"

"Yup, signed and returned, Captain, what's up?"

"Good. Here's the deal. KinCo is going public and Chase is taking over as CEO."

"Holy Crap."

"I know. If we can keep his nose clean and this IPO launches well, we are back in business, girl."

There was a pause and Kate could hear Lindsey exhale. "That's good news, Pipes."

"Yeah."

"You can't hold a good woman down. And, hey, when it's all over, can we rub it in Donna Ogrodnick's dumb face?"

"Wouldn't that be nice? But, no, we don't rub," said Kate. "Winning is enough." She felt a simmering prick of anger at the mention of her old boss' name. Kate worked for Ogrodnick for six years before she'd had enough and quit. Ogrodnick would say fired, at least, to anyone that would listen, but Kate always took the high road. When she went out on her own, Ogrodnick made it her mission to spread rumors and assassinate Kate's character. The irony was never lost on Kate. She couldn't do her job to help other people redeem themselves and save their reputations when her own reputation was being slaughtered. Kate felt a new flush of determination rise in her belly. "I've got to go. I need to get to the office and get to work."

"It's Saturday, Kate."

Kate blinked. "What? Shoot. That's right." Her mind raced. She couldn't lose two days when she only had six weeks on this job. "Okay, Lindz, thanks. Send me anything else you find."

"You got it, Pipes."

Kate slammed down a cup of coffee and rushed to the shower. She dressed, grabbed an apple from a KinCo gift basket on the kitchen counter, then made lists of all the things she needed to get done. Most important, she had to tie down any budding PR issues that might be lurking with Chase Kincaid. And the only way to do that was to talk to the man himself.

Kate took one final look at herself and tried to tame her hair. Her curls loved it here. The air in Oklahoma was like steroids to her follicles. She sighed and stepped out into the morning light.

Across the way stood Chase's identical brick bungalow, broad and flat, with an inviting front porch. Kate walked around the meandering sidewalk and up the steps to his front door. She took a deep breath and knocked.

She hoped he was up by now, even though it was Saturday. She hoped he was decent. Okay, maybe she didn't hope he was decent. He could be lounging in a pair of pajama bottoms and no shirt. She felt a little tingle at the thought. She knocked again.

"He's not home," a voice said behind her.

Kate turned to see a pocket-sized woman with bleach blond hair and red lipstick. "He's at the shop with Bo," the woman continued.

"Oh," said Kate, disappointed. "I was hoping to see him today."

"Well, I can take you down there. I'm taking the boys by to see Bo, anyway." The woman gestured toward another bungalow. There was a pickup truck in the driveway with three kids sitting in the back.

"Sure," Kate said. "That would be great, thank you."

They walked to the pickup and Kate used the roll bar to pull herself up into the passenger seat.

"I'm Sallie, by the way," Sallie said, pulling the seat up so she could reach the pedals. The truck started with a rumble. "And these are our boys. Jack is the tiny one, then Paul, then Thomas there is the oldest."

"Hi," said Thomas, toying with a giant camera strapped around his neck. Paul played with a video game without a word, and Jack stared at her wide-eyed from his car seat.

"I'm Kate." She smiled at the kids.

"Well, Kate, hope you like country music and a lot of chatter, 'cause you're gonna get both on this ride."

"That's fine with me, let's go."

As they pulled out of the driveway, Kate wondered how Chase would react to her injecting herself into whatever he did on a Saturday morning. She told herself it was necessary. Anything could happen in the next two days.

Chapter 6: Chase

Chase wheeled himself out from under a 1967 Pontiac GTO. Like every Saturday morning, he met Bo in their shop to work on their babies. He sat up and wiped his hands on a towel. Fitz, seeing he was out from under the car, came bounding over, panting and wagging his tail. Chase gave him a rub around the ears and stood up. He surveyed their new collection. There were two rows of cars, half lying in skeletal piles, the other half gleaming with fresh paint and chrome. The GTO closest to him started out a dented, limping mess. He and Bo had rebuilt the entire car, piece by piece. Today, he had finished her up by re-enforcing the chassis and testing the pistons. She should purr like a kitten now. He cleaned a smudge off the chrome and admired her angles. "Looks good, Bo," he said.

"Yup."

"We might need to take this one onto a back road later and see what she can do."

"Yup."

"Too early for a beer?" Chase asked.

"Never too early."

"Thought so." Chase walked to the shop fridge and pulled out two cold ones. He took a long, refreshing pull from one and set the other on the hood of the '67 Chevy Camaro RS. "How's it going?"

"Good. She'll be ready for the new engine tomorrow and we can take her for a spin."

Chase had a satisfied smile. He felt more at home in their little shop than almost anywhere in the world, except maybe the manufacturing floor of KinCo. Here, he was able to filter the speed of his world down to a drip. When he concentrated on the cars and their engines, all his worries dropped away.

It had been this way since high school when he and Bo discovered their shared interest in cars. They started tinkering on three wheelers and dirt bikes before they could legally drive. Bo didn't care if Chase was the boss' kid, and because his parents were farmers, they didn't want Chase to do anything for them. The two of them could just escape into the mechanics of an engine.

Bo was a tank of a kid, even at fourteen, but he still tore up and down the back hills of their town on the back of a dirt bike. They both soon discovered that Chase could go a lot faster, which they both chalked up to "drag." Chase watched Bo's big body, half bent over and buried in the cave of the Camaro's empty carcass, and smiled. "Are you gonna be able get out of there by yourself?"

"Yup." Bo grunted.

Chase knew that yup really meant screw you, and he smiled even wider. He really needed a Saturday morning in the shop with Bo this week. His stress level had been at an all-time high, and he constantly felt like he was going to trip and fall into a pile of shit. He wondered why it was when he was so close to realizing his dreams he had the greatest fear of everything falling apart. If he could just keep everything as it was and on pace, everything would work out. He tried to keep telling himself that.

As he tried to get a handle on his nerves, he thought about Kate Piper. When he found out she was a Reputation Manager there to manage *him*, he chaffed more than just a little bit. But there was something reassuring about her presence. He was glad he would have at least the weekend to reconcile these two emotions.

Aunt Peggy was right. He was attracted to her and had a hard time hiding it. *Don't screw this whole thing up on the two yard line, Chase,* he told himself. *You can keep it professional, right?* He thought about her sitting across from him, so direct and open, her shoulders, her curves, her luscious lips slowly explaining how she would help him. He thought she was attractive on the road, but he had no idea how the reality of just talking to her would affect him. She had a tone and a confidence he found intoxicating, but reminded himself she had a particular skillset, that's all. She was managing him, for Christ's sake. He was suddenly relieved he had a couple of days away to compose himself and come up with a game plan on how to keep his distance.

"Hey, y'all," he heard Sallie's voice bellow from behind him. Right on time, Chase thought, bringing the boys to say hi to their dad on a Saturday morning. "I have a visitor for you, Chase."

Chase turned and found himself locked in the bold blue gaze of Kate Piper standing in the sunlight of the bay doors.

"Oh, hell," Chase murmured. What was she doing here? He was completely thrown by the sight of her standing here—here, in his garage, looking so fresh with her tousled hair, white V-neck t-shirt, and jeans. His memories of her didn't do her justice. She was breathtaking. He felt his plan to avoid her fading away. He couldn't escape her, and worse yet, he didn't know if he wanted to.

"I wanted to continue our talk from yesterday," Kate called out to him. "And you weren't home."

It struck Chase that she had been assigned the empty bungalow right across from him. Their doors, their beds, just one hundred feet away from each other. He wondered how he'd ever sleep again knowing she was so close by. He shook his head to gather his wits.

"Ms. Piper," Chase said. "This is a surprise." He ran his fingers through his hair and looked around the room, suddenly worried what his Reputation Manager would think about his hobby and hoping she didn't take a good look around.

"Kate," she said. "I'm just Kate." She shrugged. "It is Saturday, after all."

They looked at each other silently across the room and everything seemed to slow down. Dust floated softly in the light from the windows and Chase saw a genuine smile bloom on Kate's beautiful face.

"Bo!" bellowed Sallie, "Get out from inside that engine and help me with these kids."

"Yup," Bo replied. He stood, put down a wrench and moved to the truck to get the little one out of the car seat.

"Hey, Dad," said Tommy.

"Hey," Bo replied, and tousled Tommy's hair. He set up the car seat on a work bench, while the middle kid ran to a nearby set of chairs to continue playing his video game.

"I'm gonna go outside," Tommy said, holding his camera, "see what I can find."

"Okay, Son."

Bo walked over to Sallie and looked down. He towered over her by at least two feet. "Hey, baby," he said, picking her up and kissing her on the mouth.

Sallie grinned and threw her arms around his neck. "Hey, sweetie." She clutched his face in both hands and smiled, then hopped back down to the ground and gave Bo a playful smack on the rear. Then she turned to Chase. "Chase, where are your manners? Aren't you going to invite your new friend in? Offer her a drink? I know you weren't raised in a barn."

"Right," said Chase, happy for some direction. "Kate," he said, and her name felt good on his lips, "would you like a—a beer? Hell, I think we have water in here somewhere."

Kate grinned. "A beer would be great. When in Rome, you know."

Chase looked relieved. Maybe Kate Piper wasn't some uptight East-coast skirt after all. He grabbed a beer out of the cooler and handed it to her. He felt the same electricity he felt every time he got within five feet of her, and decided maybe it was something he'd have to deal with, even if it made him uncomfortable.

"What's all this?" Kate asked, using her beer to point up and down the row of cars.

"Just a little hobby. Bo and I like to find and rebuild these beauties."

"And race them?" asked Kate.

Chase felt his heart screech to a stop. He knew it. Here we go, he thought. The inquisition. She was going to try to chain him to his desk. "Now that would be reckless. No, we only drive these girls for fun."

He saw Bo's face perk up and turn towards him. Chase ignored him.

"Really," said Kate, deadpan. It was a statement, not a question. She walked up and down the row of cars in various states of assembly. "Where do you find them?"

"Different places," answered Chase, following just behind her. "Internet, estate sales, other collectors. Bo takes care of most of that."

Kate glanced at Bo and he nodded in assent.

"And then, what?" asked Kate. "You rebuild them?"

"Something like that," said Chase. "We take them apart to see what they're made of, then we put in parts we have, replace others, and make our own."

He watched as Kate bent down, appraising the angles of the cars. She ran her fingers along one broken fender with a fresh light in her eyes.

"Why? Why do you rebuild them?"

He thought for a moment, putting his hands on his hips. He'd never articulated why he rebuilt these cars. No one ever asked him before. Finally, he answered. "In the end, we like to think we've made something better. That we improve the lives of these little cars."

Kate smiled. "That sounds noble," she said.

"I suppose." Chase said, reminding himself to be on guard. This woman was here to control his reputation which meant control him. "You said you wanted to continue our talk from yesterday," he said coolly. "Let's get that done."

He thought he saw a little frown pass Kate's lips, but she nodded and said, "Yes, let's. Is there a place we can speak privately?"

Chase motioned toward the back door which led them to a small patio. They sat across from each other in two worn wooden chairs shaded by a giant oak tree. Fitz padded out behind them, circled twice then sat at the side of Chase's chair with a sigh.

"Who's this?"

"Fitz. He runs the place."

"He's cute." Kate smiled, then withdrew her notebook and flipped through her notes from the day before. Chase sat in silence, anticipating what would come next. He considered the possibility that she was playing nice while she gathered ammo before she laid the hammer down. He frowned at the idea.

Kate looked up at him as if she were about to say something, but saw the look in his eyes and paused. She tapped a pen on her leg, then bit the end of it as she studied him. Chase watched the end of the pen touch her lips and wished she'd stop doing that. He shifted in his chair and waited.

Kate looked out beyond the patio at the flat expanse of fields and blue sky. "Nice place," she began. "Tell me about growing up here."

Chase furrowed his brow. Was she trying to trick him? "Pretty normal. Company town. Good people."

"Not to me," she said. "This is totally different from my childhood."

Chase saw something screw up in her eyes, but then she shook it off.

"Was it tough growing up as the boss' son?" she asked.

"Sometimes," he answered.

"How so?"

"Well," he took a swig from his beer, "When I was younger, I thought people liked me."

"Didn't they?"

"Maybe." He shrugged. "But I could never be sure. I learned pretty quickly that when they were nice, they were about to ask for something. Or their parents were. I don't blame them. KinCo is the only major employer in the area, and getting close to me might have seemed like a good way to get a leg up." He reached down to pet Fitz, who rolled over on his side appreciatively. When he looked up, Kate was looking at him, her gaze unwavering and intense.

"That must have been hard," she said.

"I adapted."

"And girls?" Kate continued. "I'm sure they liked you."

Chase laughed. "Yeah, sure enough. And I liked them right back."

"Any that could pop-up and cause problems? Produce photos, make any allegations?"

Chase tensed and remembered the purpose of this little talk. "Nope. I squashed anything that could be a problem years ago."

"How so?"

He shifted, resigning himself to the idea that even though this conversation was uncomfortable, it was necessary. Kate had a job to do and he knew well enough already she was tenacious. Better to get all of this over with.

"Look," Chase began, "I was a normal kid. I met girls, went to parties." He hoped he didn't look as uncomfortable as he felt. "But it became pretty clear in High School that the girls were more interested in *talking* about hanging out with me than physically hanging out with me."

Chase saw Kate raise her eyebrows.

"I thought when I went to college that would change. Went to bigger parties. Met more girls.

But by that time, everyone was obsessed with taking pictures and video of absolutely everything, and pretty soon, I was being tagged in photos by people I didn't even know." He frowned. "Like I said yesterday, I'm private. I didn't like it."

"As far as I can tell, so far, you've covered yourself pretty well. We couldn't find you in much social media in the last seven years."

"With a lot of effort." Chase gazed at her. "I've had to—well, isolate myself."

"I see." Her brow furrowed.

Chase scoffed. "Don't feel sorry for me, Kate. I have it easy. I'm privileged—I know that. I have a great family, and a company I love. I don't mind giving up some things to make sure all of that is safe."

Chase watched her smile and nod her head. Somehow, just looking at her made this whole conversation easier. He couldn't remember the last time he was this open with anyone.

"I hope you know I'm here to help you protect this life. After all the effort you've put in to having pretty much no public reputation, I don't mind you being a little irritated that I'm here looking over your shoulder."

"But you're my bumper." Chase grinned.

"Right." Kate nodded her head and laughed.

She looked across at him and Chase saw something so real in her eyes. He hoped he wasn't fooling himself. "What about you?" Chase asked. "Why do you do this?"

"What? Reputation Management?"

"Yeah."

She took a drink from her beer and looked out at the sky. "Let's say I know what it's like to be maligned for no good reason. Sometimes good people are shoved into a box they don't deserve. I like to help them get out."

Chase nodded, then joined her in looking up at the changing sky in silence.

The door opened and Bo came out. "Sallie says barbecue back at the house," he said simply.

Chase and Kate watched him duck back under the door and leave.

"Hungry?" Chase asked.

"Starving," Kate admitted.

"Let's get some food then." Chase stood and held out his hand.

Kate looked up and took his hand. God, she was beautiful. And totally not what he expected after yesterday's meeting. As they were walking out, Chase maneuvered Kate past the other bay door, the one that was closed with another set of cars behind it. He hoped Kate wouldn't derail him, but until he knew for sure, there were some things he would keep to himself. He was attracted to her, he accepted that grudgingly. But that didn't mean he would trust her.

Chapter 7: Kate

Kate sank back onto a wooden chair on the far side of the lawn and looked out at the early night sky. The sun had dipped below the trees in streaks of sherbet orange and pink, and she could see the sliver of a new moon shining between some distant clouds. There was a scent of grass and soil that had been blazing in the sun all day, now letting out its final gasp before resting in the cool dark of the evening. The sidewalks were lined with tiny solar lights, and in a bank of trees on the edge of the house, fireflies darted in an out of sight. Kate felt transported to a fairytale land she had never imagined.

She saw Chase walking toward her with two glasses in his hands. She felt the rush of energy sweep along with him as he approached, another strange sensation she was getting used to here in Oklahoma.

"Sangria?" Chase asked as he offered her a glass, then sat down next to her.

"Yes, thanks." Kate took a sip. Red wine, lime, and… was that brandy? Whatever it was, it ran down her throat in a wave of heat to her belly. "Yum," she said.

"Yeah, that's Sallie's special recipe."

"This, too? After the brisket, potato salad, and pie, I thought she'd be out of special recipes."

"Oh no, not Sallie. She lives for a good barbecue."

"She's good to have around, then."

"Definitely."

Kate and Chase sat together looking out at the evening light. Bo and Sallie were sitting in another set of chairs closer to the grill, and their kids were running around in the grass. The little one was on his belly, patting the grass with his hands in wonder. Kate got a sudden pang in her stomach, remembering her own family. She could still remember how wonderful nights like this could be, even if they were on the neighborhood block in the city instead of here in the country, with open sky and crickets chirping.

Kate turned to Chase. "This is certainly not what I expected when I hunted you down today."

Chase turned his body toward her and feigned

surprise. "What? Don't you know this is how we treat all our guests in Oklahoma? We wear them down with kindness and a great dry rub until they are putty in our hands. That's how the West was won."

"Well, then, consider me putty."

Chase grinned. "Oh, I will."

He gazed at her, looking a bit conflicted. "Kate, I have to apologize. I was not the nicest person when you got here."

Kate raised her eyebrows in response.

Chase continued. "I've been a little on edge, as you can imagine."

Kate instinctively reached out and touched his leg. She saw a spark of desire and surprise in his eyes, and immediately withdrew her hand. "That's alright," she said. "I give you a pass for the first day."

Chase rubbed his hands roughly against his thigh where Kate's hand had just been. "In my own defense, I had good reason to be skittish when we met on the road."

"Oh, really? Why's that?" She lowered her head and looked up at him with a scowl. "Did I look dangerous?"

"No, actually…I hate to admit it," he said, "but just a few days before you got here, I found a truly crazy person on the road."

Kate laughed. "What do you mean?"

"Seriously. I was on my way to the office and

he waved me down. I thought he had car trouble."

"Okay…"

"So, I get out and he's just real fidgety. Keeps checking me out and checking out my car…" Chase stopped and looked down. "I can't believe I'm even going to tell you this part."

"Go on."

"Well, it got pretty strange. He was a little guy, I asked him if he needed help, he looked around and then…well, he shoved me."

"What?"

"Yeah, weird, right? He shoved me. I took a step back and he lunged forward and he shoved me again. Finally, I pushed him back. He fell on the ground and I got in my car and drove away. There are crazy people in the world, so, like I said, I had good reason to be wary when I saw you parked on the side of the road."

Kate felt the hairs raise on her arms. "Lone guy. Side of the road, and you pushed him to the ground."

Chase looked at Kate and realized she didn't think the story was funny. "Yes, Kate, because he pushed me, like a crazy person. I pushed him away from me and got in my car and drove away."

"Was he alone?"

"Yeah."

"Are you sure?"

"What? Yes. I mean, I didn't see anyone else." Chase shook his head. "Is this how it's going to be now, Kate? Everything I do will be questioned and second guessed?"

Kate saw that old look returning to Chase's eyes, the one filled with suspicion and distrust. *Dammit,* she thought. *I'm losing ground*. "No, of course not." She forced herself to smile in a casual way. "That is a crazy story. What a weirdo."

Chase studied her for a moment, then exhaled and nodded. "Yup. Not just in Boston, huh?"

"Guess not."

Kate willed herself to take a deep breath of the evening air and relax. She had almost forgotten who she was and why she was here. She didn't get evenings like this, surrounded by friends and fun, and a great looking man she could barely breathe around. She would go back to her real life tomorrow. Right now, she felt protective of this moment.

She looked over at Chase and he turned his eyes on her. Kate thought they must have both been thinking the same thing because they both smirked at each other. She heard herself giggle and raised a hand to her face. Just then, a quick flash of light enveloped them. They looked over at Tommy, kneeling on the grass. He was holding his camera before his face. "That was a good one," he said, before running off.

"We're caught," Kate said, "having too much

fun." She nodded towards Tommy. "Does he always carry that thing around?"

"Yeah, ever since Bo gave it to him about three years ago, I've never seen him without it. He's got a lot of talent, actually. Wants to be a professional someday."

"That's nice."

Chase turned his gaze on Kate. "I would've loved to have seen you as a kid, Kate."

"Oh, yeah?"

"Yeah. Little Katie Piper." He gazed at her curiously "What were you? Daredevil? Know-it-all?"

Kate shook her head with a laugh. "God no. I was a scaredy-cat."

"No way."

"True. I was terrified of everything."

"I don't believe it. Like what?"

"Everything. Storm clouds. The ocean. One time we went to the mall and I had a fit, insisting my parents make everyone get off the escalators. I would have been very happy to curl up in a dark room and never leave." Kate smiled, remembering. "But my mom was having none of that. Oh, no. You're scared of the water, Kate? Swimming lessons. You're scared of the vacuum? Well, now you're in charge of vacuuming the house."

He stared at her in mild disbelief. "Your mom sounds amazing," Chase said.

"She was," she said as she gazed off into the distance. "My mom always said, 'Kate, be true to yourself, do the right thing, and everything will always work out'."

"Good advice."

Kate nodded. Those words always ran through her head, but so far, she hadn't found them to be true. She still hoped, though.

Chase moved closer to her and Kate watched as his hands reached out and touched hers. She could feel his eyes on her face, her mouth, as she looked up at him. He searched her eyes as he drew closer, then his lips were on hers. She felt herself surrender to the pull of his body against hers as a rush of desire washed over her. "Wait," she said, pulling back in shock. "No, no, no. Bad idea."

Chase leaned back, but didn't let go of her hand. "Why, Kate?" He looked deep into her eyes. "I like you. And," he lifted her chin to meet his gaze, "I think you like me, too. What's the harm in getting to know each other better?"

"Is that what we're doing?" she said, fear surging suddenly in her veins. She shouldn't have told him that story. What was she thinking, opening herself up like that?

Chase sighed and pulled back slightly, a look of caution in his eyes. "I don't know, Kate. Maybe this is a bad idea. You are a pain in the ass. And bossy." He reached out and grazed the back of her fingers softly with his. "But, you are also amazing, and sexy as hell, and I just don't see the harm in spending some time together."

Kate felt a fizzy warmth rising in her body, mingling with the fear. She tried to squash the desire and concentrate on the danger. "But everyone can see us."

Chase looked around at the other bungalows, soft lights glowing in their windows. "Well, I'm not sure if you've picked up on this, but the local perception of me is that I can be a little uptight. Hell, they probably think a little fun would do me good."

Fun, Kate thought. Right. That's what this was. And fun would do nothing to get her closer to her goals. She had been on her own for half of her life and learned that depending on others only brought her heartache. She felt a terror that letting herself kiss Chase again, to fall into the abyss of his arms, would only cause her pain.

Kate took a breath and pulled away. "Wrong place and time, I think." She patted the back of his hand. She could see that the patronizing gesture hurt him, but that was probably for the best.

She watched as Chase's eyes changed from confusion to determination. "Alright," he said. "Let's make it the right place and time. How do people normally meet these days?"

"Don't be ridiculous."

"No, seriously. On-line dating? Grocery

store?" He smiled boyishly. "Clearly a barbeque didn't do the trick," he said with a wave of his hand.

For a fleeting moment, Kate wanted to change her mind. She wanted to say okay and fall into his arms. How wonderful that would be, she thought, if only for a few days. He did make it difficult to say no.

"Afraid not," she said, trying to sound as certain as possible. "Another life, maybe." She felt tears begin to well up in her eyes and hoped Chase couldn't see. If he did, he would break her.

"Oh, I get it," Chase said, with a nod of his head. "You want a love story. A prince and a ball, and everything."

Kate wanted to say don't be ridiculous, but deep in her heart she did want a love story. She just knew she was never meant to have one, and to even try was a recipe for disaster. She gave him a shrug. "Guess so. Hard to please. Better for you just to slide that glass slipper on another girl's foot."

Chase stood and looked down at her as he sunk his hands into his pockets. The night stood still as Kate listened to the crickets chirp and watched fireflies glide in and out of the trees. He was gorgeous here in the moonlight, and Kate vowed if she couldn't have love, at least she would always have this moment. Chase made no move to leave, so Kate said, "Goodnight, then."

Chase nodded. She could swear she saw a smile playing at the corner of his eyes.

"Be careful what you wish for, Kate Piper." He bent down and kissed her on the cheek and walked away.

Chapter 8: Chase

Early Monday morning, Chase closed the door to his bungalow with a soft click and padded down his front steps and across the lawn. There was a low buzz in the trees and grasses of rural Oklahoma as a soft, low light awakened the earth. Tiny droplets of water began to slowly evaporate on the blades of grass surrounding the walkways and flower buds stretched to life.

Chase loved this time of day. He felt like anything was possible—that each morning gave him a chance to start again, and today, he felt particularly hopeful. He practically pranced across the compound to Kate's house and tip-toed up her steps. He didn't see a light on and wondered if she was awake or still curled up inside the bedsheets. He avoided the temptation to knock on the door, knowing he would see her soon enough.

From his jacket, he withdrew a small, cream colored envelope labeled simply, "Kate", on the outside. He smiled at himself, gave the envelope a little tap for good luck, and then slid it beneath her door.

Chase was used to going after what he wanted, and he didn't often lose. Last night, he decided that what he wanted was Kate Piper. He wasn't accustomed to chasing after women, and the whole prospect made him a little uncomfortable, but after that kiss, he couldn't allow himself anything else.

As he got into his truck to drive to work, he replayed that kiss over and over in his mind, just as he had the whole night before. He remembered how the soft pads of her lips slid over his, her tongue touching his tongue, her arms slung around the back of his neck as her body pressed onto his. He wanted that again, and more. As he played it over again in his mind, he tried to put his finger on another simmering sensation lingering deep inside the kiss. The way her skin seemed to melt into his and how he felt them both being totally transported to another place. He had never felt anything quite like it.

He admitted to himself that he was stung by her rejection after the kiss, and how vehemently she pulled away. He couldn't blame her, though.

Her job was to disintegrate entanglements, not create them. Plus, he had only known Kate for two days. He didn't know if becoming involved further would intensify or relieve his stress. And, at the end of their work together, he knew Kate would be gone. The idea already pained him. He didn't know what would happen with Kate, but he knew couldn't let her leave without investigating these feelings he had for her.

As he entered his office, he looked across at the chair Kate had sat in during their first meeting. He shook his head and smiled. What a crazy few days it had been. First, he found Kate on the road, worried she was some kind of spy. Then, he had turned her into a simple fantasy, before finding out she was to be his new reputation manage, after which, she admonished him like a child.

Then, they shared that kiss, that wonderful kiss. Chase felt like he had whiplash. Three days ago, he thought his whole life was on track, and the machine of the IPO would propel him into next month unscathed. Perhaps it would be better not to have captivating Kate Piper thrown into the mix, but part of him felt a tug he couldn't deny. A desire to wrap Kate back into his arms and sink back into that faraway place together. He didn't know how he had been so overcome by his feelings in just a few short days, but he wanted to take a long, warm bath in whatever made up this amazing, surprising woman named Kate Piper.

Chase turned on his computer and brought up his calendar in an effort to clear his head. He had to find a way to segment Kate—to relegate her to one corner of his mind, or he would never get anything done. He struggled to concentrate on the screen before him. Peggy would be here first thing for a meeting to go over the latest financial projections, so he boned-up on a couple of spreadsheets before the meeting began. Chase knew it was never wise to let Peggy see you come to a meeting unprepared. He learned years ago that Peggy was more on top of her game and her job than anyone else at the company, except maybe him. She worked hard, and if she found anyone else not putting in appropriate effort, she considered it a personal insult.

Peggy had given up her own life to the KinCo machine. She had never married, and had given her youth to catapult KinCo to the national brand that it was. Most people found her bitter, but Chase just found her to be dedicated. He sometimes wondered if they were destined for the same fate.

There was a knock on the door and Peggy entered.

"Good morning, Chase."

"Good morning. Coffee?"

"No, already had four. Ready to go over some numbers?"

"Absolutely. Have a seat."

Peggy sat and crossed her long skinny legs beside the chair like a gazelle. She laid a portfolio full of documents on the desk, with tabs and sticky notes sticking out in uniform fashion along the edge. "Before we begin, I have a couple of housekeeping items I'd like to discuss."

"Go for it."

"First, the Governor has asked key members of the board to meet with him before his gala next week. We will need to arrive in the morning. I've made all the arrangements."

"What's that about?"

"Good news, I think. The governor is rolling out a new jobs agenda before the launch of next year's re-election campaign and it looks like he's going to pitch a KinCo partnership."

"That's fantastic."

"It is. Great exposure. We'll learn more when we get there, although I'm preparing a myriad of data so we will have whatever he needs available."

Chase smiled and folded his hands on the table. "I'm sure you are."

Peggy continued. "Also, I have invited our Investment Bankers to the Gala. They will be here from Japan, and I think the Gala will illustrate how strong we are in our community, and in partnership with our local government."

"I agree."

Peggy took her eyes off her notes and gave Chase a fiery look. Uh-oh, Chase thought. Something is brewing. She's gearing up for a fight.

Chase prodded her. "And? What else is going on?"

Peggy un-pursed her lips and exhaled with a slight shake of her head. "Some new information has come to light about our temporary Reputation Manager."

"Kate?"

"Yes, *Kate,*" Peggy sneered. "I know that Cal usually has a good eye for these things, but I took it upon myself to do a little digging after her unexpected appearance Friday. After all, we didn't know anything about this woman. I'd never heard of her, had you? Then she just pops up here and expects us all to trust her with the biggest deal of our lives."

Chase sat silently, ready for the assault he felt sure was coming.

"I will try to be as kind as I can," Peggy continued, "but suffice it to say, she has a *shady* history."

"Shady? In what way?"

"Well, apparently, she almost destroyed one person's athletic career after exercising astoundingly poor judgment during his ordeal. She has been described to me as a loose-cannon with questionable ethics. Some say she slept her way up to her last job. I believe that, too, because she also, apparently, has a criminal history. If she didn't sleep her way to the top, how else could she have gotten a pass to work with so many successful people and companies?"

Chase sat perfectly still and watched Peggy spew out accusations until all of the air left her like a spent balloon. Then he responded. "Hm. That's strange, Peg, because Cal said she came highly recommended."

"By someone she slept with, no doubt."

"I find that hard to believe. Where did you get this info?"

Peggy straightened her arms against her knee, and lifted her chin an inch higher. "I know a lot of people, you know. Just because I've been stuck in Oklahoma my whole life doesn't mean I haven't cultivated my own sources."

"I see." Chase was troubled by these accusations, more because Kate was saddled with rumors like this than the likelihood that they were true. He knew Peggy distrusted most people, and sometimes rightly so, so he decided not to disagree with her outright. "Okay," he said. "We'll keep an eye on her work. But, just remember, she's only here until the launch, then she's gone."

"Thank Heaven for small favors," Peggy said. "Now, the numbers…"

Chase listened to Peggy review the data in

silence as he mulled over her words. His sense of Kate didn't jive at all with the accusations Peggy just foisted. He decided he would give her the benefit of the doubt and hoped she wouldn't disappoint him.

Chapter 9: Kate

Kate emerged from the steamy hotel shower and put on the fluffy full length robe hanging from the bathroom door. She wrapped her damp hair up into an enormous white towel, then opened the bathroom door to let the steam escape before pouring herself a glass of wine. She padded over to the seating area of her hotel suite and sank onto the couch to video-call Lindsey. Lindsey's face popped up after one ring. Kate thought she must have been sitting at her computer, as always.

"Hey, princess, getting ready for the ball?" Lindsey asked.

For a moment, Kate regretted telling Lindsey about the conversation with Chase and the note he'd slipped under her door. But she checked herself and smiled. She *was* excited. Last Monday, she found a tiny cream colored envelope pushed under her front door. When she opened it, she was surprised to see these words:

A Ball it is. Please, put on your glass slippers and meet me there.
Details to come via email.

She had woken up that Sunday morning full of regret about her kiss with Chase the night before. She wanted to literally pound her head into a hard surface. How could she be so careless? So reckless? So stupid? But then she saw the note and felt a twinge in her heart.

The email came with the details of the Governor's Gala, including information on the car service that would be driving her to Tulsa, and how to check-in to her hotel room. She had to call Lindsey right away to ask her to overnight a couple of dresses. It had been two years since Kate had worked on a job that warranted attire for this sort of function, and she had to ask Lindsey to crawl back into the dusty recesses of her storage unit to find a group of dresses, shrouded in plastic covers.

Kate smiled at Lindsey through the camera. "It's just a political event. No big deal," she said, but couldn't contain the enormous grin that spread across her face.

"How fun!" Lindsey said. "I assume Prince Charming will be there."

"He invited me, so I think that's a safe bet."

"Which dress did you choose?"

"The black one. Low cut but full length, so still professional, I think.

"I was hoping you'd choose that one. It's my fav. Call me before you go so I can see you."

"Okay," Kate said with a smile.

"Now," Lindsey continued, "before we get too carried away with girlie stuff, there have been some developments I need to loop you in on."

"Oh?"

"Yeah, well, nothing crazy, just weird."

"Weird how?"

"Well, I created an alert on Chase's social media history—the ones with those ancient pics and posts other people had made about him. Since I created the alert, most of the files have been removed."

"That wasn't you, right?"

"No. Looks like someone else has been cleaning up. I messaged a couple of the people who posted the original pics and they said they couldn't discuss those pics or Chase. Tight lipped, like they had signed a non-disclosure."

"That's not good."

"No, but usually when that happens, I find the pics are re-blasted through another site. But this time there's total silence." Kate watched as Lindsey furrowed her brow and tapped her keyboard, glaring at her screen. "Is it possible someone else at KinCo is making a preemptive move to get these pics off the web?"

"Not that I know of."

"Huh. Well, there's something else, too. Remember that lady that was hit during a race a few years back?"

"Yeah."

"Records say she agreed not to sue KinCo for the accident if they dropped stalking charges against her."

"Stalking charges?" Kate sat up.

"Yeah, apparently after that Most Eligible Bachelor piece came out seven years ago, Chase had more than a handful of zealous fans. This lady took the cake, apparently. By all accounts, she ran out onto the track to get closer to him."

"Jesus Christ."

"I know. But that all seemed like old news, right?

Kate felt a pit in her stomach. "Dare I ask…?"

"I tried to contact the lady to see if anything else would percolate, and she told me to contact her new attorney."

"Her *new* attorney?"

"Right. If this case was all settled years ago, why would she need a new attorney?"

"Good question. Seems like trouble is

brewing."

"Maybe. That's what I've got for now. I know you'll do your crazy voodoo and piece it all together. I'll find whatever else I can to help."

"Thanks, Lindz. I guess I should go do my hair and stuff now."

"You're going to be gorgeous, Pipes!" Lindsey said with an air kiss and signed off.

Kate took another sip of her wine. Why would someone be gobbling up old pictures and witnesses if they didn't want to release them and discredit Chase? Someone was out there planning something, she was sure of that now, she just had to stay ahead of them.

Kate took another deep sip of her wine then went to get ready for the gala. Even though she was here for work, she couldn't help wanting to have a good time. Tonight, all she wanted to do was dance, drink, and feel pretty. There would be time enough tomorrow to figure out the puzzle. And she was excited to see Chase, too. Every time she remembered that kiss, or thought about even being in the same room with him, she got butterflies in her stomach. *Calm down, Kate,* she told herself. *This is not your first rodeo*. But then again, it was the closest she'd ever gotten to a prince inviting her to a ball. She put on her dress and twirled around. She couldn't wait to get downstairs and find Chase.

Chapter 10: Chase

Chase felt an eager tug at his heart as he looked at his watch, then scanned the ballroom again. Still no Kate.

Soft music played from a small orchestra by the stage, and the ballroom was bathed in a soft yellow light that floated down from the chandeliers and up from the candlelit tables. Chase watched as groups of people weaved in and out of the ballroom and onto the dance floor. He took a sip of his champagne then placed it back on the table.

Chase had gotten great news before the gala. The Governor offered to partner with KinCo on a new jobs initiative to revitalize stagnant parts of the state with manufacturing jobs. The State was offering job training and tax-free infrastructure loans if KinCo could guarantee another ten thousand jobs to unemployed Oklahomans. Cal and Chase had been working for months on how to build the best infrastructure to sustain all the new products they would have to produce once they went global. Everything was coming together so perfectly it was like the universe telling him he was on the right path. He felt giddy, and all he wanted to do was share it with Kate.

Kenji Kai was also at the meeting with the Governor. He led the Investment Banking team underwriting KinCo's Initial Public Offering, and even though Chase had several prior meetings with the man, he was never able to get close to him. He almost always stayed encapsulated in his group of employees and translators. Tonight though, as the Governor laid out his jobs plan, and the translator whispered into the banker's ear, Chase saw him nod approvingly and took that as a sign Kai was reassured that his belief that KinCo could support an international brand was not misplaced.

Kai had Asian distribution contacts KinCo did not, and his support was crucial to driving the international results KinCo deserved. In exchange, the board agreed to launch the IPO in Japan, but when they looked at the numbers, it was a small concession. Even though Kai's dark-eyed stare had an unsettling effect on Big Cal, Chase saw the look of a hunter in the man's eyes and he liked that. He recognized it. Kai liked to win, and Chase was glad they were both invested in the same goal.

Chase looked across the room again and was surprised to see his Aunt Peggy laughing and talking with a member of Kai's team. Chase wasn't sure what her role was, but she and Peggy looked like two schoolgirls giggling in a corner. Chase was glad Peggy had found a friend. She sure needed one.

A heavy hand landed on Chase's shoulder. He turned around to see Lou Tarly facing him with a broad grin and large open arms. "Lou," Chase said, and hugged the man. "Good to see you."

Lou kept both sturdy hands locked around Chase's upper arms as he beamed at him. "Son, I couldn't be more proud of you if I were your own dad. Cal's told me what an amazing job you've done with the company," then he leaned in with a whisper, "and will continue to do, no doubt." He gave Chase a thunderous pat, then released him.

Chase had known Lou Tarly since he was a kid. He was the family's Estate Attorney by trade, but more than that, he was one of Big Cal's life-long friends and closest confident.

"Listen, Chase," Lou said. "I understand you all have brought on the services of Kate Piper, am I correct?" He didn't wait for Chase to respond, but instead looked at Chase sternly and leaned in. "Listen to me, now. You cannot be in better hands. I *know.* Now, you might hear otherwise," he looked around the room, "there are parties with an ax to grind, but no one, *no one* is better than Kate Piper. I've seen her at work, and she's the best."

"I don't doubt it," responded Chase. "She's very impressive."

"Oh! Good. Well, Cal thought you might be a little, shall we say, truculent, as we know how independent you are. I'm glad you've seen her merit."

"It's hard to miss. She's…" Chase shrugged. "Persuasive."

"That she is, Son, that she is. Well, I'm going to go find another drink and then a bathroom. Maybe not in that order."

He slapped Chase again on the back and walked into the crowd.

Chase scanned the room once again and took another sip of his drink. To his right, he saw Peggy approaching with a blond in a white dress, a giant blue sash slung across her chest.

"Chase, this is Tandy Hill, our most recent Ms. Oklahoma."

As Peggy let go of Tandy Hill's arm she nudged the woman forward just a bit so she was standing right up against Chase.

"Ms. Hill," said Chase, offering his hand. A

gala photographer jumped in front of them just as Ms. Oklahoma dropped Chase's hand and slid her arms around his back as she leaned into him. As the flash sparked in his eyes, Chase could feel Ms. Oklahoma arch her back and raise her chin to give the photographer just the right angle. Chase instinctively dropped his head and pulled away. Just as he did, he saw Kate.

She was standing twenty feet from him, still as a doe, watching.

Chase felt his breath catch in his chest. Her dark hair was piled high on her head with just a tendril weaving down around her long, soft neck. Her gown seemed to catch all the light in the room and Chase saw her actually glowing. She was stunning.

"Kate," Chase said as he moved forward, linking his arms into hers. He wanted to look in her eyes and tell her how beautiful she looked, but she moved past him.

"You're missing the light," Kate said directly to Ms. Oklahoma.

Ms. Oklahoma's eyes darted around as she frowned. "What?"

"You can't just depend on the flash from the camera. You have to angle towards the main chandelier over there."

Kate winked at Chase then turned again to Ms. Oklahoma. "That light will age you. Better get some better pictures or those will be the ones in the paper tomorrow."

Chase watched Ms. Oklahoma flush with terror as she ran after the photographer.

Kate took a glass of champagne from a tray and smiled at Chase. "You look nice," she said.

Chase swallowed and took a breath. "You look amazing." He moved forward and took the champagne glass out of her hand. He set the glass aside and gazed into her eyes. "I'm so glad you're here." He laced his fingers through hers and led her to the dance floor. His other hand slid around her waist and landed decisively on her lower back, pulling her close to him. Their bodies pressed against each other as Chase began to move her slowly across the floor, his eyes never leaving hers.

He saw her struggle, trying to look away, but then she sank into his embrace and met his eyes. He was holding her so close he could feel her heart thundering in her chest.

He pressed his cheek to hers and breathed in the scent of her hair, lost in the slow, rhythmic sway of their bodies moving together across the floor. He'd felt that same sensation when he kissed her, that the world was churning away and disappearing, rolling into a faraway oblivion where nothing existed but him and Kate, his body and hers, and the bond he felt when they were close.

His eyes felt hot and his mouth dry as he

pulled away just enough to see her eyes. "Kate," he began, but the song ended and a voice announced the Governor was about to speak. "Later, then," he said. "There's so much I want to tell you."

Kate nodded and squeezed his hand. They walked arm in arm back to their table and Chase felt the whole world open up before them. He started making plans for what he would say and do, and how he would win Kate over and make her believe that this feeling had to be right. He squeezed her around the waist again as they got closer to their table, but as they approached, Kate stopped dead. Her body went stiff and Chase felt everything change. He looked at her and saw a cold dread had enveloped her face. She was staring toward the table and the woman Peggy was speaking to earlier.

Chase put his arm around Kate again but she pushed it away firmly, taking a step away from him. He watched her back straighten and saw her take a breath to compose herself as a woman's voice cackled softly. "Well. You do get around, Kate Piper."

Chapter 11: Kate

A cold shudder ran through Kate's bones. She had let her guard down, just for one night, and before her stood Donna Ogrodnick. *I deserve this,* Kate thought. *I should have known better.*

She did her best to draw herself up, and willed her lips to curve into something like a smile. "Donna, this is a surprise."

"*You're* surprised?" Donna asked. "I thought you were long gone by now. Still slogging away, trying to get some clients, I see?"

Kate felt Chase by her side and his heat reassured her, even though she was terrified of the optics. Donna would twist this around for sure.

Chase reached out his hand. "Hi, I'm Chase, and you are…?"

"I was Kate's old boss, isn't that right, Kate? Until we had to...part ways."

Kate had played through this moment a million times in her head, shadow-boxing Donna Ogrodnick so she'd be ready with something witty to say when they were face to face again, but now, when she searched her mind, it was empty. A blank desert of nothing but fear.

"Are you a Reputation Manager, too?" Chase asked, saving her. "I wasn't aware."

"Oh no," said Donna. "I'm a Crisis Manager. The big leagues."

Just then, Kate got her voice back. "What Donna means to say is that she comes in after a life is already destroyed and tries to tape the pieces back together. I, on the other hand, find it more valuable to help clients ward off disaster before it strikes. It might pay less, but it's more rewarding." Kate took another sip of her champagne. "From an ethical standpoint."

Kate saw Donna bristle. "Well, to each his own," she said. "If you're here working with KinCo, that means I've been hired as back-up, for when you're well-meaning hand-holding leads to total disaster." Then she turned to Chase. "Don't worry, Chase, I'll be here to help you pick up the pieces."

"That won't be happening," said Chase. Kate wanted to reach down and squeeze his hand but didn't dare.

"Maybe not through you," Donna said, looking the two of them up and down, "But I've been hired by Mr. Kai to ensure your public reputation stays intact after the launch. He is investing a lot and has my firm on retainer. Should the unthinkable happen, he wants a pro by his side."

Just then, Kate heard another voice. "Oh, Donna, this is a tired old act." Kate turned to see Lou Tarly at her side.

"Lou," she said in surprise and hugged him, happy to have his thick, reassuring arms around her. "What are you doing here?"

"Old friends with Big Cal. Didn't he tell you?"

Suddenly, Kate knew it had been Lou that had recommended her to Cal. Someone from Boston still believed in her.

The lights above flashed, signaling the Governor was about to take the stage. The group disbanded and went to their different seats around the table. Now that they were sitting, Kate felt the room begin to spin. She took another drink of her champagne and reached below the tablecloth and took Chase's hand in hers. He squeezed her hand reassuringly and she saw him looking at her, worry etched on his face.

Kate looked across and saw Donna Ogrodnick at her table sitting between Peggy and Kenji Kai. She felt adrenaline pulsing through her veins. If she failed now, everyone would know, Donna

Ogrodnick would make sure of that; no one would ever take her seriously again.

"Ladies and Gentleman," a voice called over the sound system, "It is my pleasure to introduce..."

Kate felt blood rushing through her limbs and gripped the sides of her chair in an effort not to run toward the door. Scenarios swirled through her mind as the ballroom lights dimmed, and she struggled to keep her face benign. She pulled her hands back up to applaud the Governor as he took the stage, trying to keep them from shaking.

"Thank you all for being here tonight," the Governor said from the podium. "Tonight, we are here to celebrate the fact that the American Dream is alive and well in the great State of Oklahoma. No matter who you are, or where you come from, with hard work..."

His words muted and mixed in Kate's mind. As he spoke, she felt her adrenaline continue to rise. She took a long drink from her champagne and tried to slow her breath. The second the Governor's speech ended, Kate sprung from her chair and darted across the room.

She wrung her hands and tried to calm herself down. She felt completely powerless, completely out of control. Donna Ogrodnick was never going to stop until she was destroyed. Everything she'd worked for, all those years of struggle, would be for nothing. She saw Donna laughing across the room, whispering in people's ears. She was whispering to Peggy, and now to Cal and Rose. Kate's heart pounded in her chest. She saw Chase parting the crowd and moving toward her, concern in his eyes. He took her by the hand.

"Kate?" he asked. "What's going on?" Kate shifted back and forth on her feet, looking over Chase's shoulder. Chase grabbed her by both shoulders and made her look him in the eye. "What's going on?" he asked again, and this time, Kate looked into his green eyes. Her body and mind were so tense that she desperately craved an escape. She looked at Chase's lips and arms and knew she could find comfort there.

Kate grabbed Chase by the hand and pulled him out into the hallway and down a second vacant corridor. She took his giant hands and pressed them into her waist, then reached up and curled her hand behind his neck, pulling his lips down to hers. Chase pulled back, looking at her, his face questioning. She wanted to be transported from this place and from this fear. She felt a hunger flood through her, and the recognition of it in Chase's eyes.

"Kiss me," Kate said, and any reservation Chase had left his eyes. They crushed against each other, their lips pressed together, sliding, searching as their tongues touched and their breath quickened.

As Kate pulled Chase against her, she could

feel his erection growing and straining against his pants. She pressed her torso against him and moved her body slightly, hearing him exhale in her ear. His hands were on her, moving up and down her waist then over her breast. He moved one hand up her thigh and towards her core, and she could feel the heat radiating from within her.

"Upstairs," Kate said between kisses. "Now."

Chase took her by the hand and they maneuvered through the hallways, across the lobby of the hotel, and to a waiting bank of elevators. As soon as the doors closed, they were on each other again. Kate took the palm of her hand and rubbed it across the bulge in his pants as she took his mouth in hers. With a ding, the elevator doors opened and Kate found her room key. As she inserted the key in the lock, she felt Chase behind her pressing into her back, his lips on the back of her neck, his hands grasping around to squeeze her breasts through her dress. She felt a clenching between her thighs and a spring of moisture which begged to be touched.

They tumbled into the room, almost falling. Chase grabbed her by the waist and held her up. He pushed her against a dresser, again taking her mouth in his. Then he withdrew, his breath ragged as he looked at her. "Kate," he began, but Kate put her hand across his mouth and said, "Shhh." Then she kissed him again.

He raised her dress up around her waist, then

trailed his hand up her thigh between his erection and her panties. His fingers cupped her, then moved beneath the fabric. She knew he could feel how hot and wet she was as his fingers slid up and down, circling until he found her clit. Her head fell back as a moan escaped her lips. He slid his finger inside of her, and she felt her muscles clench around it, wanting more, wanting all of him inside of her.

Kate slid away from him and walked over to the bed. As she looked at him, she reached to her side and unzipped her dress which fell in a pile around her ankles. She watched his eyes taking her in as she reached up and pulled the pins from her hair, which fell around her shoulders in a splash. He came at her then, taking her around the waist and pushing her onto the bed. Kate crawled back across the covers. "Take off your clothes," she whispered huskily.

Chase stepped back and undid his tie, his eyes never leaving hers. He took off the cummerbund of his tuxedo, then pulled his shirt out and undid the buttons. As he opened the shirt, Kate felt a new wave of desire. His skin was so smooth and taut, and she couldn't wait to feel his bare skin against hers. She watched as Chase slid off his shoes and undid his pants, which he stepped out of, unleashing a giant erection, which Kate wanted inside of her immediately.

Instead, Chase crawled towards her on the

bed, sliding his hands up and down her inner thighs, spreading her before him. With a final look of desire washing across his face, he bent down and began to lick her. His tongue immediately found her clitoris and Kate felt electricity flood her brain. Her back arched and she pushed herself toward him, her body starting to swirl in motion with his tongue. He freed one hand and reached up to cup her breast, kneading her nipple between his thumb and finger as his other hand flattened on her lower belly, pulling up just enough to expose her sex for his mouth. The tip of his tongue circled her deftly, and as she swelled at the touch, a ragged moan escaped her lips. Then he took his hand from her breast, and as he licked her, he slid two fingers inside of her. Her body exploded into a symphony of sensations, growing, crashing, rising, until she felt herself come to a crescendo, her muscles pulsing around him.

Chase sat up with a satisfied grin, his lips wet, his hand still gently caressing her slippery folds. He eased himself on top of her, kissing her slowly, desire thick on his mouth. He looked at her beneath him, "Kate," he whispered, his voice laden with emotion, and Kate felt something besides desire stir inside of her.

She slid one leg around his and flipped him over, pinning him beneath her. "Shhh," she said. "Don't do that. Don't say my name." She reached across the bed for her makeup bag, from which she withdrew a small foil wrapper. She felt Chase's eyes on her as she opened the package with her teeth, then slipped a condom over his erection. She looked up at him, watching him flush as her hands slid up and down along the length of him, his breath ragged as he stiffened in her hand.

She crawled above him, her sex lingering just above the top of his, teasing him with her hand, sliding him back and forth across her lips, wetting him. Then she lowered herself down, enveloping him, and she felt her muscles expand and then clench as she took him deep inside of her. Her eyes closed and her head dropped back as she began to pull herself up and down, slowly taking him in, deeper and deeper.

She heard him moan slightly as he took her by the waist and pushed her down even farther, their two bodies sharing the same root, her hips now moving rhythmically with the push of his hands. She leaned back, riding him, feeling in total control, her hands lying flat against his torso, pushing off of him, grinding into him.

When she opened her eyes, she saw Chase looking at her, his eyes moist and his mouth slightly open. As their bodies moved together and their eyes locked, she felt a bonding she did not want to feel.

Chase began to say something again, so Kate

bent her body forward, covering his mouth, breaking any contact beyond their two torsos moving as one. She could control this. She began thrusting herself onto him, deeper and faster until she felt him grow inside of her, his hands clutching at her ass, tension mounting as their bodies climbed in sync. Then she heard a groan escape from Chase's throat and she clenched in response, a wave of heat crashing down from inside of her body and surrounding him as he climaxed inside of her, grasping at her back and saying her name. "Kate," he said breathlessly. "Kate…"

She laid across his chest, their breath rising and falling in sync. As the moment lingered, Chase wrapped his arms around her and gently kissed the tip of her shoulder and arm. Kate pulled away, and as she felt him slide out of her, a sick feeling came over her.

She curled her shoulders inward as pain pierced her heart. She had let herself feel too much, and now she was adrift. She had lost on both sides. She was no longer in control and had become everything Donna Ogrodnick had always accused her of: sleeping with a client to get ahead. Is that what she had done? Kate felt emotion swirling through her balled up stomach as she took a deep breath to try to sort her thoughts. She clutched a sheet around her and pulled even farther away.

Chapter 12: Chase

Chase rolled to his side and squinted at the slice of light that peaked out beneath the heavy hotel drapes covering the windows. It was difficult to tell the time, but he knew it was still early when Kate slipped silently out of bed and tip-toed to the shower. For most of the night, she had curled herself into a tiny ball on the corner of the bed, as far away from him as she could get. Chase kept trying to inch closer to her, to hold her, and finally Kate had allowed him to put one hand on her back as her chest rose and fell, the breathing of someone awake and waiting to run.

He ran his hands roughly over his face as he tried to replay the events of last night. When Kate walked into that Gala, he literally felt the earth stop rotating. The light clung to her and she stood, glowing, as the music and crowd faded into a foggy distance. When Chase wrapped his arm around her and looked into her eyes, he felt like they were in a fairy tale. He wasn't expecting to end up in her hotel room. Chase ran his hands across the sheets then pulled them up in his fists as he looked over toward the bathroom door.

He didn't know what had freaked Kate out last night, but clearly it had something to do with Donna Ogrodnick. He would have to do a little investigating of his own and find out what the story was there. Whatever the reason, he knew Kate had taken him upstairs as a release. Usually, he would be just fine with a woman wanting him just for sex, but Chase felt a pang of fear that this might be the only time he could be this close to her. And it wasn't what he wanted. He felt a profound need to make love to Kate, to hold her, to look in her eyes and connect with her and know her.

Chase heard the shower turn off, and several minutes later, the bathroom door opened with a rush of steam. Kate walked out in a hotel robe, her wet hair starting to curl loosely around her shoulders. She looked up with a timid smile then crossed her arms, putting her weight on one leg.

"You're still here," she said, looking at the floor.

Chase tried to discern if she was happy or irritated by that, but he couldn't figure out the look on her face. "Is that a bad thing?"

"No. No...I just—I thought you would have gone to your own room by now. To get your stuff. Car service should be here soon."

He searched her face, hoping to see some affection there. "I can order the car. Twenty minutes, okay?"

"We're taking the same car?"

Chase rose from the bed, letting the sheet that had covered him fall away, and he stared at her. "Don't look so disappointed."

Kate hesitated before she responded, her eyes lingering over him, and then she looked away. "That's fine," she said. "No problem. Twenty minutes is great."

He watched her gather her things, avoiding his stare. Finally, he reached down to grab his pants and shirt, which he put on in silence, then walked to the door. "Meet you downstairs," he said, and walked out.

Chase texted the car service on the way to his room, admonishing himself all the way. He showered and changed, then gathered his things. As he did, he felt a weariness rise up inside of him. Kate was exhausting.

As he walked into the bright light of the lobby, he saw their black town car waiting at the curb outside just as Kate was stepping into the back. *Wow,* he thought to himself, *she just can't wait to get out of here.* He left his room key on the lobby counter and hoisted his bag over his shoulder.

"Chase," a voice said behind him. He turned to see Donna Ogrodnick.

"Lovely event last night," she said, "although you seemed to have missed a large part of it."

Chase leveled his gaze at her, unimpressed. "What do you need, Donna?"

Donna raised her eyebrows with a half-smile. "We're all short on sleep and a little cranky today, it seems, but I come to you as a friend and ally, if you'll have me."

"Get to the point."

"Fine. Kate Piper."

"What about her?"

"As I mentioned last night, Kate was in my employ for some time, and I feel it my duty to warn you that she displays a pattern of behavior that's, well...predictable and unfortunate."

Chase clenched at the strap of his bag. "Being?"

Donna leaned in conspiratorially. "Amongst other things, she tends to…how do I put this? Make herself *available* to her clients in a very personal way, if you get my meaning. Maybe it's to get control or manipulate them, who knows? But in our business, it's very bad form. Muddies the waters." She reached out and put her hand on his arm reassuringly. "We're all adults here, but I tell you this just so you know all the angles and can protect yourself."

Chase moved his arm so her hand fell away. "I don't need your warnings, and let me be clear, you're implications are unwelcome."

"Well," Donna said with a shake of her head. "I've said my piece. Do with it what you will."

Chase watched her walk away. *No wonder Kate hates that woman,* he thought. He turned toward the door and saw Kate looking at him sadly through the window. As their eyes met, she sunk back into the dark interior of the car as the shaded windows rose up, enveloping her.

"Shit," Chase muttered to himself and walked outside.

As he slid into the backseat of the car beside her, Kate looked straight ahead, her arms and legs turned away from him. The car pulled out and onto the highway, they each looked out their windows in silence for a long time. Chase looked over at her and saw turmoil roiling over her face. He could only imagine what was going through her mind. "I had fun last night," he said.

Kate smiled politely. "Me too."

"Your dress was beautiful."

"Thank you."

"Kate, listen, I—"

"Chase," she interrupted, "something's happening."

"I know, I feel the same way."

"No," Kate shook her head. "Listen, I should have told you last night. Something's happening with your launch."

Chase sat back, stunned. "What are you talking about?" He leaned forward and pressed the button to close the partition between the back seat and the driver.

"I don't have anything concrete yet, but let's just say, I'm finding some disturbing trends."

"Like?"

"Like people purchasing old pictures of you. And that woman… the one you hit on the raceway? She has a new attorney."

Chase felt sick. "Why? What are you talking about? Why would someone stir that up again?"

"I don't know. Not yet, but we need to be alert. That means being one hundred percent on our game. No distractions." Then she looked at him, and Chase felt a sudden realization. She was making an excuse not to see him again. He nodded his head in a deliberate way. "I see, Kate. You know, if you don't want to see me again, you can just say so."

He saw surprise in Kate's eyes. "No, that's not what I'm saying." She shook her head. "Chase, I don't know…I can't—"

"It's okay," he said. "I'm a big boy. You're right. There's a lot at stake for me and I can handle a little rejection." He laughed. "It could have been good though, Kate. It could have been great."

Chase saw tears spring to her eyes and he

thought maybe she did care about him. He moved across the seat and took her hand. Although she would not look at him, she squeezed his in return.

"Kate," he said. She turned to face him and he reached out his hand and gently touched her cheek. She raised her eyes to his and he saw fear behind them, but also something else. At least, he hoped he did. He ran his hand over the side of her head, tucking her curls back behind her shoulder, his thumb running along her cheek and jawline. He saw her lips part slightly and he bent forward, taking her face in his hands, and kissed her. Her hands wrapped around the back of his neck and she kissed him back, fully. Chase felt hope spring inside of him as he pulled her to him, but then he felt her hands pushing his chest, pushing him away from her.

"Stop," she said, wiping her mouth. "Stop. We can't. I need you to not do that, please."

"No," Chase said, shaking his head. "You can't put this all on me. You were kissing me back. Just like you were last night. This is not just going to go away."

Kate turned to face him. "Did you arrange for us to have the same car hoping this would happen?"

"Maybe, but you want this to happen, too."

She shook her head. "No," she said. "No. You make me feel like I'm out of control. You make me feel like someone I don't want to be."

Chase sunk back onto his side of the car. "I don't accept that."

"Chase, listen. You have worked all of your life to run KinCo. It's your dream. And my dream is to have a successful company of my own. Neither one of us can afford to be distracted."

"This is not a *distraction* for me."

Kate turned her beautiful blue eyes on him, clearly trying to blink back tears. "I know, I know. Let's just get through the launch, okay?"

Chase shook his head bitterly. All these years he had convinced himself he had to be alone to run KinCo—that he couldn't have his career and a relationship, too. And now, he had found someone that changed his mind and all she wanted was to devour him in a hotel room, finish her job, and leave. Maybe Donna Ogrodnick was right—this is what Kate did. She slept with her clients to control them, or get a thrill, and then she was off to the next job.

Chase saw Kate's hand resting on the seat next to him and longed to reach out and hold it again, to hold her and tell her how he felt, but it was useless. Kate would finish this job and leave, and he needed to make sure he had his life, or at least pieces of it, still in place. Then he'd have something to cling to. Something to focus on besides Kate Piper.

Chapter 13: Kate

Kate threw down a couple of aspirin with another glass of water. Her head was pounding. She wondered how she could still have a hangover the next afternoon, but decided she deserved a hangover—and much worse. She put on the most comfortable pajama bottoms and fluffy socks she had in her suitcase, along with a white tank top, then piled the full weight of her hair up on top of her head in a loose bun. She scooted up to the breakfast bar in her bungalow and opened her laptop to video call Lindsey. She stretched out and rocked her neck back and forth as the phone rang. There were few spots on her body that weren't sore.

Lindsey's pixie face popped up on her screen. "Hey, Pipes."

"Hey."

"Ooh. Someone looks like they had a rough night. Bad time at the gala?"

Kate shook her head. "Where do I even begin?"

"With the dress, of course. You forgot to call me so I could see you in it."

"Right, sorry. Yeah, the dress was good. Thanks again for sending it."

Lindsey beamed into the camera. "And I bet Mr. Gorgeous was to-die-for in a tux. Am I wrong?"

Kate felt a flush and grinned at the camera.

Lindsey's eyes widened and her mouth dropped open. "Oh my God, Kate. You slept with him?"

"I did."

"You slut."

"I know."

"I'm jealous," Lindsey said, pulling a bottle of wine into view and pouring herself a glass. "Tell me every detail. You know I live through you."

"It was…unexpected."

"Ooh, so did he get all alpha-male on you and take you like the sexy beast he is?"

"Kind of the other way around, actually."

"Holy crap."

Kate nodded.

Lindsey looked at Kate admiringly. "You're my hero. Can I be you when I grow up?"

"Believe me, you don't want to be me. I

screwed up. I never should have let that happen."

Lindsey put her wine down and stared at Kate. "Are you nuts? He's gorgeous. And single. When do we ever find that combo?"

Kate shrugged.

"Do you like him?" Lindsey asked.

"I do," Kate admitted.

"Now," Lindsey continued, "this does screw up our plan of growing old together, two old coots sitting on a porch talking about how we didn't need a man. But I can fend for myself, I guess. So, what now?"

Kate looked down. "Nothing now. It's all a mess. I screwed up, Lindz, and at the absolute worst time."

Lindsey's brow furrowed. "What's going on, Kate?"

Kate exhaled, and tears flooded her eyes. "She was there."

"She who? Wait…Oh crap. No. Way. Donna Ogrodnick?"

Kate nodded.

Lindsey slapped both of her hands down in front of her. "That bitch. Is she stalking you?"

"I don't know. If I thought I could get away from her tentacles by coming all the way to Oklahoma, I was wrong. Apparently, she's knee deep in this deal. She's working for the investment bank who's launching the IPO."

"Holy crap." Lindsey said.

"If I screw up this job...If I miss anything, she'll be right there to let everyone know. Any chance I had of building my business would be gone." Kate took a sip of her water. "Every time I manage to get a client, she swoops in behind me and tells lies about me until my credibility is decimated. And her favorite line—that I sleep with my clients—has been a total lie. Until last night."

"Crap."

"Right. I just became that girl. The one she accused me of being all along."

"Now, hold on there, Kate. We know Donna Ogrodnick will tell whatever lie works best. You don't have to worry about her. If you weren't a threat to her business, she wouldn't be coming after you. Remember that. Remember who you are."

"Right." Kate sniffed.

"Okay, dumpy. Tomorrow we work on our strategy. Tonight...there's only one thing that will make this situation better." Lindsey ran off screen and came back with a small black speaker. "Dance party!"

"No..."

"Oh, yes. It's a kitchen dance party." Music began to thump through Kate's computer and she watched Lindsey adjust her camera and stand up, clap her hands, and beckon Kate to stand up, too. "Come on, Piper. Get your groove on."

Lindsey's smile filled up the lens and then she backed up, shimmying her hips. Kate felt a smile spread across her face and she exhaled with a laugh. "Okay, Lindsey," Kate said as she stood. Her shoulders and hips began to rock with the beat of the music. She did a twirl and raised her arms high over her head.

"Shake it, girl!" Lindsey yelled. "Dancing queen!"

Kate moved back into the kitchen, listening to the music, her head bobbing and her feet moving. She felt the stress leave her body as she gave it up to the music, the moment, and her best friend shaking her ass on her computer screen. Kate spun around and shimmied at the camera. Then there was a knock on the door. Kate froze.

"What's that?" Lindsey asked, turning off the music.

Kate turned and looked at the front door. Chase was looking at her through the glass, smiling. "Oh, no," Kate said. "He's here."

"He, who? Oh...*him*, him."

"I've got to go, Lindz."

"Don't do anything I wouldn't do. On second thought, do everything I wouldn't do." Lindsey grinned and the screen went black.

Kate closed her laptop and paused to try to compose herself before turning to the door.

Chase stood on her porch in jeans and a t-shirt. She saw a smile spread across his face as she opened the door.

"Am I interrupting something?" asked Chase.

Kate tried in vain to push her hair into place then crossed her arms tightly. "Dance party," she said.

"Dance party? You were having a dance party in your kitchen?"

"It's a thing," she said simply, then looked down at Chase's hand.

He lifted up a bag. "Your makeup bag. Apparently, you were so anxious to get out of the hotel this morning you left it. They delivered it."

"Oh, thanks," she said, blushing. She looked behind him at the other quiet houses lining the compound, she saw no one and opened the door. "Would you like to come in?"

Chase paused. "For a minute. Are you worried someone might see me coming over here?"

"No, I guess not."

"If I wanted to sneak over I'd just use the tornado shelter," he said, breezing past to sit at the kitchen counter.

"What shelter?"

"We are in Oklahoma," he said. "When my grandparents built these houses, each got a tornado shelter, and the shelters are connected by a series of underground tunnels. I used to play down there when I was a kid."

"Oh," she murmured as what happened last night begin to weigh heavily on her mind again.

She watched as Chase walked over to the counter and leaned against it, one well-muscled leg crossing over the other. He was so at home here, hanging out in her kitchen. She fought the urge to go over and wrap her arms around him. "I'm sorry about how I acted this morning."

"Are you?" Chase set his intense eyes on her.

Kate puffed out her breath. "There is something between us. I'm aware. We slept together within a week of knowing each other, for Christ's sake, but I'm trying to do you a favor. I don't want you to be hurt."

Chase turned his gaze on her and his shoulders relaxed. "That's it? That's your spiel?"

"Huh?"

Chase walked around the kitchen and directly toward Kate. She took several small steps back until she was up against the counter. "Don't do me any favors, Kate," he said, leaning closer, whispering with a husky voice into her ear. "Do you have any idea how hard it is for me to work so close to you as it is, and after last night, to be right across the lawn from you all day, knowing how you feel in my arms? How much I want to touch you?"

His minty breath was warm on Kate's cheek and the need to turn and feel his mouth on hers was so urgent her chest ached.

She turned her mouth to speak but Chase pressed her lips closed with his thumb. "See you at work," he said, and walked out the door.

Chapter 14: Chase

"Wow," Chase said into the phone as he looked out across the KinCo complex. "Are you sure?" The night shift was loading trucks under the glowing overhead lights. One by one, Chase watched as they shook themselves awake and rumbled off into the night. "Thanks, Lou. I sure will. Thanks."

As Chase placed the phone back into its cradle, he could hear a vacuum running down one of the distant office hallways. Under the single lamp on his desk, he began to scribble circles and squares slowly on a yellow legal pad. The lines began to intersect and overlap, and he found his pen drawing deep, twirling cylinders across the page. He wondered if Kate was still there, dancing in her kitchen. He drew the pen roughly across the page, scratching through the lines, then balled up the paper and threw it away. His eyes lingered on the balled up paper for a moment before his leg shot out, sending the trash can across the room.

That afternoon, he had paced around his house, trying to stop himself from standing at the window to look across at Kate's bungalow. He failed. As dusk fell across the compound, a soft light glowed from her kitchen, and Chase wondered if she was in there—if she was thinking of him.

Fitz watched him from a corner of the room and let out a whimper now and then, but Chase didn't respond. He was replaying every word Kate had said the night before, trying to find some hidden meaning. The soft sheen of her skin flashed across his mind and how it glistened as he ran his hands across her body. How she had clung to him and cried out as their bodies moved perfectly together—and how she turned away immediately after.

She had warned him, she said they shouldn't be together. What if she was right? He shook his head. No, he couldn't let himself think that. Her fear of being with him made her so paranoid she started to imagine there was a plot against him. Chase couldn't blame her. She was probably sensing his duplicity. Her reaction was his fault. If he'd just come clean, he could fix everything.

There was a knock on the door, and Chase rushed to answer it so quickly, Fitz didn't even have a chance to bark. There was a delivery man standing on his porch.

"Kate Piper?" he asked.

Chase frowned. "No, she's across the way." He pointed, then saw a bag under the man's arm. "Is that hers?" Chase asked, grabbing it. "I'll take it over."

The delivery man grasped the other side of the bag and looked up at Chase, both of their knuckles wrapped around a corner. Chase towered over the man and scowled down as he said, "I'll sign. Let go."

This was the excuse Chase needed to see her. He ran through what he would say. He would lay all his cards on the table. Kate could stomp on them if she wanted to. At least he would have come clean. He told Fitz to stay, then darted out his front door and straight across the lawn.

As he raised his fist to knock on the front door, he saw Kate there in the light of the kitchen, dancing. His arm dropped. She looked so happy, so free. He wished he could make her look like that, but as he stepped back into the shadows of her front porch, he knew his revelation would knock that beautiful smile off her face. He couldn't tell her.

Chase braced himself, then knocked on the door. Just as he feared, he saw Kate's face drop when she saw him. He gave her the bag but left without saying what he came to say.

There was a heavy moon hanging in the sky as he jumped into his truck and sped off onto the back roads of town, the feel of the accelerator below his feet and the soothing whir of the tires and engine calming his mind. He found himself at the entrance to his office, not remembering exactly how he had gotten there. He walked inside, nodding silently at the security guards and stepping into the elevator. When he reached his office, he walked directly to his desk and began to rummage through some business cards stuck in a back corner. After flipping through a dozen, he found Lou Tarly's number.

It was late in Boston, but Chase couldn't wait until morning. After several rings, he heard Lou's deep, scratchy voice come on the line. "Chase?" Lou asked. "Is that you, Son? Is everything alright?"

"Yeah, Lou," Chase replied. "I'm sorry to call you so late, but I have questions only you can answer."

Twenty minutes later Chase felt the fizzy tendrils of new emotions stretching and combining in his mind. He leaned back into his chair and made himself breathe. Kate. Beautiful, amazing Kate. After what he learned, he knew he never wanted to be without her. But he knew he couldn't tell her the truth.

Chapter 15: Kate

Kate was tucked into a corner of Big Cal's office, watching a group of sales guys that had gathered around his desk.

"Cal," one said, "tell us about time before the internet."

Each of the guys had collected his Friday cookie tin from Constance and was sitting or standing around Cal, hoping to get a classic bit of Cal's wit before heading back to work.

"Son," Cal replied, "people actually had to talk to each other back then. None of this *text-ing* and *app-ing*. You would have been in sorry shape. You actually had to *talk* to girls. Face to face." Cal reached out and slapped the man playfully on the arm.

Kate had snuck in hoping to find Chase. He couldn't be found and had been clearly avoiding her the whole week. Last night, the windows to his house remained dark. When she stopped by his office, all his staff would say was that he was in an off-site meeting. *He's trying to give me some of my own medicine,* Kate thought. *Serves me right.*

"Cal," Kate heard another sales guy say, "I heard you drove market to market to get orders, even when you knew you didn't have the product to sell them."

"That's right."

"Without inventory?" the guy asked in shock.

Cal smiled. "Well, back then, we took the orders on a paper form with carbon copies attached to a clipboard. It took weeks to fill an order, not days. That gave Rose a chance to work her magic in R&D and figure out how to make what they needed. In all our years, we never had to turn an order down or say we couldn't fill it."

A ticking sound popped against Cal's office window. Everyone looked up and saw Rose standing on the other side of the glass, smiling at Cal. He took his foot down and straightened up, his head tilted to one side. Rose raised one eyebrow, withdrew a tube of red lipstick and drew it across her lips slowly, never leaving Cal's stare.

"Um, fellas," Cal stammered, "I think my wife would like to have a word with me. You all skeedaddle, now."

Everyone got up with a smile and a smack on the back of their neighbor. Kate followed. "Hi, Rose," she said as she exited.

"Kate," Rose replied, her stare never breaking with Cal's, then she walked into his office, shut the door, and dropped the blinds.

Kate walked over and leaned on Constance's desk, both of them looking at the closed door.

"Wow," Kate said.

"Uh-huh."

"Have they always been like that?"

"For forty years."

"Huh," Kate said. "I didn't know love could be like that after forty years."

"Yup."

Kate looked back at Constance's desk, which was now devoid of cookie tins. "How long have you been doing this cookie thing?"

"Pretty much forty years," she said simply. "I like to bake. Takes my mind off things."

Kate felt a ding on her phone and looked down. Lindsey was calling. She stepped away from Constance's desk to take the call. "Hey, Lindz, what's up?"

"Kate. I just got a ping on my alert system. I don't know the details, but it looks like Chase was in a crash."

Kate put her finger to her ear, trying to hear Lindsey more clearly. "A crash? What do you mean? What kind of crash?" Kate saw Constance raise her head.

"There was just a quick story on the wire. A Chase Kincaid was the driver of a car that crashed at a race in North Carolina this morning. That's all the info there is. I don't even know if it's our Chase, but given his history of racing, I—"

"I'm on my way. Text me everything you can."

Kate hung up and looked at Constance.

"Is it Chase?" Constance asked.

"Yes, I don't have details." Kate's eyes darted to Cal's office door. "I'll call you with any info I get. I'm on my way to North Carolina. Connie," Kate reached out, "Will you please let Cal and Rose know?"

"Of course," Constance said, squeezing Kate's hand. "You be safe, too, now."

Kate nodded and rushed out the door. She hurried down to the parking lot and jumped in her car, driving faster than she ever thought she would to get to the airport.

As the plane took off, tears sprung to her eyes. Please, she prayed, please, let him be okay. Please, let him be okay. A clarity came over her, white and blinding. She loved him. Nothing mattered but getting to his side.

As the plane taxied to her gate, Kate removed her seatbelt and stood.

"Ma'am," a flight attendant said, "you must stay seated until the captain turns off the seatbelt sign."

Kate sat back down, tapping her hands on her legs. She turned her phone back on and immediately got a text from Lindsey. It read, "Sorry, Pipes," and included an attachment.

Kate tapped on the attachment and a picture popped up. It was Chase in a photo from the local paper. He was laying on a gurney, being wheeled swiftly down what looked to be a hospital hallway. His face was singed and it looked as if his jacket had been cut off of him. His face was tilted back in agony, and at his side, pushing away photographers and rushing down the hallway alongside him, was Ms. Oklahoma.

The plane jerked to a stop and passengers around her began to undo their seat belts and stand to retrieve their overhead luggage. Kate stayed in her seat. She felt like all the blood had left her body.

Chase was alive, though apparently injured, but he had lied to her. He hadn't told her he was leaving town, let alone to race cars. And not only that, he had left town to be with Ms. Oklahoma.

She shook her head and wiped a tear from her cheek. She had been played. This whole time, he was flirting just to get her to back down, to loosen his collar just a little bit. He must have been. And she had fallen for it. How stupid she felt.

Well, she was still Kate Piper, and she still had a job to do. She stood and exited the empty airplane. As she made her way to the hospital in a taxi, she pushed her despair away and ran through what this exposure meant for the IPO. She texted Lindsey. "How wide is it?" she asked.

Lindsey replied right away. "It's not. Just local North Carolina outlets, so far." Then another text came. "You alright?"

Kate stared down at the text for a long time before replying. "Yes," she typed. "I should have known better."

Chapter 16: Chase

Chase reached out with his one good arm and placed his hand on the bedside table. That stopped the room from spinning. He closed his eyes and took a deep breath. When he opened them again, the light above the bed floated in a gauzy haze, and the angles in the room sank and dipped like he was sailing in a stormy sea.

Tubes ran from his arm and body, trailing across the bed covers. He was tethered to machines. The only thing he could relieve himself of was an oxygen monitor pinching the end of one finger. He pulled it off and tossed it to the end of the bed, then turned to try to find a clock. As he did, a stabbing pain shot through his shoulder and up the side of his neck. He groaned inwardly, but refused to hit the blue button to ask for more drugs. He had to keep his head clear.

He shouldn't be in the hospital. The race was just a Test and Tune. They were just there to dial-in the car, see what it could do. It was a clear morning. The track was clean. He should have known when the other driver pulled his car past the staging beam, then right back to the wet-box that he would lose traction. As soon as the light dropped, both cars shot forward, and the other car crossed the center line and slammed into him. He didn't even feel the pain until the pit crews pulled him out of the smoking car and onto a gurney. It was a blur after that.

Chase reached for a cup of water and leaned forward to sip it through a straw, but even that shot pain through his torso. "Dammit," he moaned to himself. He took another sip. He had to flush these drugs out. He wondered how long it would be until he could pull himself out of this bed and slip into a taxi to the airport. When everyone found out—and they would—he wanted to be upright and able to defend himself.

First, he had to find Kate. If he could just explain to Kate, they could figure everything else out together. *Where had Bo put his phone?* He had been so stupid. He thought if he gave himself totally to his company in every other way he could keep this sliver of his life to himself. It wasn't even real racing, after all. Just drag racing.

He never thought he would get hurt.

Chase started to feel the drugs evaporate from his limbs just a bit. As he did, pieces of the day began to refill in his mind. Inside the ambulance, as his clothes were being cut from his body, the EMT asked, "whose Kate? Whose Kate, buddy? We'll find her. Quiet now, you just lean back."

Chase gripped the rail on the side of his bed. He had to make his way back to Kate. He would change. He would tell her everything. Then he heard her voice.

"Hello, Chase."

"Kate," Chase said, turning his head toward the door. "You're here." He reached out his hand, but then pulled it back when he saw the look on her face.

Kate crossed her arms and scanned his body. "You're lucky. Just a sprained arm and bruised ribs, I hear." She advanced into the room and put her bag down near the window. She pulled a paper out from her bag and tucked it under her arm.

She was a few feet away, but Chase blinked, struggling to see her clearly. "How did you get here?"

"Airplane. How most people travel."

"No, I mean ... how did you know?"

"You can't hide forever, Chase."

He tried to pull himself up, but a bolt of pain shot through his arm. When he looked up, Kate was glaring at him.

"Try not to hurt yourself," she said in a clipped voice.

He wasn't sure how he wanted this talk to go, but he knew this wasn't it.

He took a breath. "Let me explain."

She looked at him flatly. "Okay," she said. "Explain."

In his haze, he reached up to pluck the right words from his brain. "I know I should have told you," he stuttered. "But it's complicated."

Kate didn't say anything, so he continued. "The racing, it's, well—it's the only thing that was totally mine. It didn't have anything to do with the company. I thought it was no big deal, I—"

"Everything you do affects the company. That's what I've been trying to tell you."

"I know, I get that now. I just—I want you to understand why I did it. Why I didn't tell you. I told you before, growing up in a company town as the boss' son was tough. The cars were the only thing that were mine, and I guess I got too protective of that. I—"

"Stop complaining," Kate said.

"What?"

"Stop complaining. First of all, it's annoying. Second, everyone complains so it's boring. Third, no one wants to hear it. Do you think your investors will care? Or your employees? Everyone is focused on their own problems so it's ridiculous to complain."

He fixed his eyes on her. She stood in the corner with her arms crossed, no hint of empathy on her face. "I don't understand. Where is this coming from?"

Kate uncrossed her arms and shook her head. "It's not the world's fault that you inherited a company. It's not the world's job to cut you a break or understand that you had it rough as a kid. And, it's certainly not your investors' obligation to pay for your dreams. Which is what is going to happen if your hobby tanks this IPO. Nobody wants to hear it." She picked her pad of paper back up. "So, stop whining. We have work to do."

Chase stared at her in disbelief. He tried to shake the drugs off and sit up. He recalled his revelatory talk with Lou earlier that week and shook his head. No wonder Kate was reacting this way to a car crash.

"The IPO is being announced to the public tomorrow," she said. "Everything looked good until you decided to get on the front page of the paper."

"What? What paper?"

Kate tossed the paper face up onto his bed. "Right there. You and Ms. Oklahoma racing down the hospital corridor. Now the narrative will be you are reckless. Untrustworthy. Not fit to invest in."

He squeezed his eyes shut then opened them wide, trying to focus on the photo. "It wasn't that big of a deal, Kate. It was just and exhibition, for Christ's sake. No one was killed. And I don't even know where Ms. Oklahoma came from. She was just there in the hallway when the photographer got there."

She exhaled. "This is your company, Chase, and your IPO, but I would stop saying things like, 'it's no big deal'. Your investors won't appreciate that. Especially after you've given them the impression you could die any moment in a fiery crash."

Chase felt a deep pang of regret. "You're right," he said. "What now?"

Kate came closer to the bed and sat at the very edge. Chase wished she would take his hand, but she didn't, and now he feared she never would again.

"Where's Bo?"

"He's at the track collecting the car." He watched as she punched something into her phone.

"Tell me about the car."

Chase stared at her in confusion. "It's wrecked," he said.

"I know that. Did you build it?"

"Yes."

"With KinCo parts?"

"Some. Some we made ourselves. But the parts

weren't faulty or anything. It was the other driver and the wet box," Chase slurred, as a wave of nausea washed over him.

"The *wet box*?"

"Yeah, he...got in the wet box, which helps with friction, should have made everything sticky."

Kate glared at him. "You must be joking."

"No, listen. It's all about getting out of the box." Chase made a rotating motion with his fingers.

"You are ridiculous. Seriously."

Chase took a deep breath and tried to focus. "Kate, if you just give me a chance, I can—"

"How many new auto parts does KinCo release every year?"

"I'd have to check. Dozen maybe."

"Were there any new parts you were using in the car?"

Chase furrowed his brow. "Yeah, um, we've been working on a couple of things that haven't hit market yet. New alternator. New seat belt design. Rose actually started the design on that before she retired. Kate, listen, I wanted to tell you, I did."

"So, now you've told me."

"That's it?"

"I've got work to do," she said as she stood. Chase reached out with his good hand and grabbed her forearm.

"Kate," he pleaded. "Don't do this. Talk to me."

Kate looked down at him and he could see her eyes begin to glisten. He wanted to stand and hold her and not let her go until she understood. He never would have kept this from her if he knew what she would mean to him, if he knew he could lose her.

The door to the room opened and Rose and Cal rushed in, followed by a nurse. Kate tugged her arm out of his grasp until he was trying to hold onto the very end of her fingertips.

"Oh my God, Chase," Rose said as he rushed over and hugged him. "Are you alright?"

"You gave us a scare, Son." Cal said.

Chase nodded. "I know. I'm sorry."

Chase saw Kate gather up her things and walk toward the door.

"Kate," Chase called out, "Wait..."

"You're in good hands, now," she said, then she turned to Rose. "Could I speak to you for a minute?"

Chase watched in disbelief as Kate walked out the door.

Chapter 17: Kate

The photographer met Kate just outside the shop. "Thanks for getting here on such short notice," Kate said. "I need a couple of good shots of him in front of the car. Get a few more of him around the shop, and a few more of the wreck itself."

"You got it," the photographer said. "I'll go in and set up."

Kate re-checked the body of her press release. As soon as she had the photos done, she would send it to a list of news outlets with the title, "Leading Manufacturer of Auto-Safety Parts Launches IPO." *Never let a crisis go to waste,* she murmured to herself as she walked over to her car to dial another reporter.

Streaks of gray and pink stretched across the Oklahoma sky above Kate as she took a sip of tepid coffee. She heard a rumbling noise and turned. A red pickup truck rocked down the uneven road toward her as her phone began to ring in her ear. Even in the dim morning light, she could see Chase's eyes boring down on her from the passenger seat inside. She stared back, reminding herself it wasn't her job to coddle him, it was her job to make sure he didn't destroy his own IPO. She didn't care how much he hated doing press. One photo shoot was not a lot to ask.

Chase winced as he hopped out of the truck, his arm tucked into a fresh sling. Kate took a breath. It had taken every shred of self-control she had to not throw herself across his body when she saw him lying there in that hospital room yesterday. When she learned he was alive and conscious, she felt herself exhale in deep gratitude, even while reminding herself she cared about him too much.

It was not her place to care as much as she did. She was not his family. She was not even his girlfriend. She was his Reputation Manager, and his company and her career depended on her keeping her head straight.

The reporter answered her call as Chase walked up to her. "That's right," Kate said into the phone. Chase stood in front of her, scowling. "The launch is two weeks from tomorrow. Yes, we're very excited. No, Mr. Kincaid was testing the part. Thanks to that seatbelt, he only sustained a minor injury. He believes in his product. That's right." She put her hand over the receiver and said to Chase, "Go in. The photographer is waiting for you," then went back to her conversation. "I'm sending you everything. All the stats will be in the body of the release. Yes, photos, too. Looking forward to it."

She hung up, took another sip of her coffee, and then walked through the bay doors and into the shop.

Chase stood proudly in front of the mangled front end of his race car, wearing an intrepid gaze as the photographer's camera clicked rapid-fire against the silence of the open room. She saw Chase's eyes flit to her then back away, his jaw grinding. She stood in the back and watched as he shifted from one leg to the other. "How many more?" he asked.

"Almost done," said the photographer.

Kate walked over to the camera and looked through the viewfinder. "We're good, Chase," she said, looking up briefly. "You can go. We've got your shot." Then she turned to the photographer. "Get a few more of the car and we'll wrap it up."

The photographer handed Kate his card. "Call me anytime. It's not often we get corporate jobs out here."

Kate nodded, and as she did, a thought flew

through her mind. She reached for her phone and texted Lindsey: *Find out who got the credit for that photo of Chase on the gurney. Find out why they were at that race.*

Kate turned off her phone and looked up. Chase was standing near the bay doors looking at her as if waiting to talk to her. She couldn't avoid him forever. She walked over. "Good shoot," she said.

"So, we're okay?"

"The news release will go out later this morning. By the end of day, we should have some positive press. I think we've changed the narrative enough."

"I meant us."

"What us?"

"I meant are *we* okay?" Chase exhaled and looked at her. "I know we aren't. But I'm hoping we can be."

Kate took a breath and steadied herself. "We're fine. The launch is still on track."

"Kate," Chase said sternly. "Stop deflecting. You know I'm not talking about the IPO." He took a step closer and she felt a current of energy stream over her again. She tried to step back, but it was too late, she knew Chase saw the emotion in her eyes.

He grabbed her hand and pulled her onto the back patio. As they faced each other in the morning light, a cold breeze blew across her skin.

A storm was coming in. She circled her arms around herself and shivered.

Chase slid his jacket from his shoulders and slung it around her, pulling her into him with his one good arm. Kate felt safe tucked inside his jacket. It smelled like him. She exhaled sharply as she tried to put the pieces of her strategy back in place. She needed this job to work. She needed her career. She couldn't let her feelings for Chase ruin everything.

Chase pulled away from her just enough to look down into her eyes. "Kate," he said, "I screwed up. I know that. No, don't look away from me," he said, gently tilting her chin up with his hand. "I'm sorry I lied. But I'm not the only one who's been lying."

Kate blinked up at him, then pulled away, her brow knitting together. "What is that supposed to mean?"

"I'm onto you."

Kate felt a rush of fear, but Chase pulled her close again. "What do you mean?" she asked.

He paused as if considering his next words. "You like me," he said, a smile forming at the corners of his mouth. Kate tried to pull away, but he pulled her in again, his torso flattening against her own. She felt her heart begin to race. She swallowed. "Do not."

"Stop lying. Let's both just stop lying." Chase nuzzled into her neck and said into her ear. "I don't know what this is, Kate. All I know is when they pulled me out of that car, all I could think of was you."

Kate pulled back and looked at him in surprise.

"Me? What about Ms. Oklahoma?"

Chase let out a little chuckle and rubbed his eyes. "Is that what this is all about?"

Kate ruffled. "No. Of course, not." She straightened up, even though he was still holding her around the waist. "I do find it curious she just happened to be there. I don't care, really, but I thought we were being honest now..."

"Kate, I swear to you, she just popped up. Photographers seem to be like fertilizer to a flower on that girl." Chase pulled her a bit closer again, his thighs pressing against her. "I promise you, when we go to race, we just go to race. We don't party, we don't tailgate, and we don't take pictures. It's about the cars. It's always been just about the cars."

Kate felt herself soften. She wished she could believe him, but now that the IPO was launching and all eyes were on them, she had to be more careful than ever. She pulled back. "Okay," she said. "I believe you. I have to get this release out now." She tried to pull out of his embrace, and for a moment, he held her there, his hands firm, his eyes imploring, but then he released her. "This isn't done, Kate."

"It never is with you."

"No." He smiled. "I'm going to convince you. I'll find a way."

Kate smiled back. She secretly hoped that he would.

Chapter 18: Chase

"Connie, do me a favor," Chase said into his phone, "call Kate and tell her the board would like to meet her at eleven in the conference room. No, I know the board is not in today. Just tell her that and reserve the room, okay?"

The last few days had been a blur of meetings and phone calls. The company phones were lit up by investor and press inquiries. Kate's press release had increased interest in their IPO. At this rate, they would have to increase the company valuation for the launch. Two days ago, he was afraid he had ruined his chance of going global. Today, the launch was stronger than ever, and he had Kate to thank for it. And he would have thanked her, if she wasn't totally avoiding him.

The more Chase tried to connect with Kate, the farther she pulled away. If there was one thing Chase had learned in the last week, it was that secrets could destroy them, and he wasn't the only one who had them. He thought back to his conversation with Lou Tarly before the race. Chase leaned back in his chair and shook his head. No wonder Kate was evasive. He would have been, too.

Chase felt a rush of uncertainty. Backing Kate into a corner could be the wrong move. He knew that much. But in two weeks, this launch would be over, and Kate would be gone, back to Boston and her life. He had to fix this now. No more secrets.

Chase sat waiting in the conference room. First, he chose the chair at the head of the table, then moved to one farther down. Then she could sit next to him. No, across from him. He looked at the door and then his watch. So, he was early. She would be here soon.

The door to the conference room opened and Kate stood in the doorway, looking around at the empty chairs. Her head dropped and she gave it a little shake before she looked up. "Board meeting, huh?"

Chase stood. "I know. Just—please, let's talk."

Kate walked in and laid her stuff down, then walked over and sat next to him. She smiled, that was a good start. He looked at her for a moment, trying to forecast how she was going to react. He considered reaching out to hold her hand, but thought that might make her bolt.

"Honesty is important," he began.

Kate's brow furrowed. "Honesty?"

"Is important. Yes. I know that now."

"Oh God. Do I need to be worried? Again?"

"No, I—look, I wanted to tell you everything at the hospital. To be fair, you did have me at kind of a disadvantage. I'd like to fix that."

Kate looked at him incredulously. "Alright, then. Tell."

"Okay, I'll start. First, as you know, I used to race on a track. That was too high-profile, and after that girl ran out onto the track, well, I never wanted anything like that to happen again."

"Smart."

"All that press before the accident, and after, just made me hate the whole thing."

"I can see that."

"Right, but I still loved the cars, and me and Bo…that was our thing, you know?

"Uh, huh."

"So we pulled back to do just drag racing. Just us and the cars against a clock. Honestly, I never thought I'd be injured or that anyone would even know."

Kate nodded. "I get it."

"You do?"

"Well, not the fast cars part, but having

something that's just yours. I get that. I understand why you needed that."

"Good," Chase took a deep breath, "and—hear me out now, I know why fast cars make you nervous."

He watched as Kate's lips parted and her mouth hung open.

"I know about your family, and about everything that happened with Donna Ogrodnick."

She gawked at him. "You've got to be kidding me." She shook her head. "People talk, Chase. That doesn't mean what they say is true."

"I talked to Lou."

She looked at him in disbelief. "Lou? Lou talked to you?" She shook her head. "Wow. That's great. What? You two gossiped about me like a couple of old ladies?"

"It wasn't like that. I called him. He didn't want to tell me. Know that. But," he reached out and grabbed her hand, "I told him I cared about you and wanted to know."

She tried to pull back, but Chase grabbed both of her hands in his. "Kate, you are amazing."

"You snooped into my private life?" she said, her blue eyes glistening. "You shouldn't have done that."

"Please, hear me out. I had no idea what you had gone through…what you've overcome."

"I don't need your pity. Or anyone's."

"Pity? Oh my God, Kate. I admire you."

Kate uncrossed her legs and slumped slightly in her chair. "Why? I can't even get my own company off of the ground. You…you're the one who's amazing. You run this whole place, no problem."

Chase leaned forward. "Kate, if I had any idea your family died in a car crash, I would have told you everything right away. I'm sorry."

"That was a long time ago."

"How old were you?"

"Twelve."

Chase squeezed her hand. "Lou told me there wasn't—that you—you were raised in a home."

Kate nodded.

"You still graduated from high school, put yourself through college, made a career for yourself."

Kate sniffed. "I thought I did. Then I got in Donna Ogrodnick's crosshairs."

"From what Lou said, you made a judgment call. The right one."

"Wow. You know a lot."

"I'm persuasive. Don't blame Lou." Chase rubbed her arm as he spoke. "I'd like to hear it from you, though." He looked in her eyes. "No more secrets, Kate."

As seconds passed, Chase wondered if Kate would pull away. She looked toward the door once, then sighed. "Okay. So, we had a client, pro-athlete, caught on a yacht with two underage prostitutes and a lot of blow."

Chase nodded.

"One of the girls overdosed. He called Lou, and Lou called us. We got there just as the ambulance was wheeling her out. Stringers were everywhere and we only had a few minutes to decide our play. Donna said deny everything. Burn the evidence. Lie. Say he was never there." Kate shook her head. "I said, the playoffs start next week, this guy is a key player, and we were in Boston, after all, they love their sports. I said we couldn't contain it. Better to play up that he was celebrating the season, in a bad way, yes, but because he loved Boston. He called the ambulance, but he had no idea the girls were underage. He would probably get a two-game suspension and be back for the end of the playoffs and the Super Bowl, if they were lucky.

"Donna said no, and insisted we go with her plan, which totally backfired. Pictures surfaced of the player doing lines with the girls at a local bar, and the girls had texted their friends they were on his yacht. Whole thing blew up. He got caught in the lie. You probably saw it, it was all over the news."

Chase nodded. "So you were right and Ogrodnick was wrong. That's why she was so mad?"

"No. Other clients started questioning her

judgment. She blamed the bad strategy on me, said I was mad because I was sleeping with the athlete and told him to lie. That I sabotaged him out of jealousy. All that mattered to Donna was saving her own reputation." Kate nodded bitterly to herself. "Ironic, huh? Then, everywhere I went, she told clients that I would stab them in the back. That I grew up in juvie because I was dishonest and a criminal."

"Wow," Chase said, "she is a piece of work."

"Yup. I guess if I could ever get ahead, people would start to believe me. She just can't have that. And Chase," she said, squeezing his hand back, "she is treacherous. It makes me really nervous she's working with Kai."

"I can see why."

"So, now you know everything. Still want to work with me?" she let out a small laugh. "No one else ever does."

Chase squeezed her hand, then stood, shaking his head. "Kate, I knew from the beginning I'd have to be careful."

"What does that mean? You don't trust me now?"

He chuckled. "I knew I had to be careful because I had convinced myself I'd have to be alone to run this company. Then you breezed in and changed everything." He stroked her cheek. "When you got here, something in me cracked, Kate, something changed. I knew I'd have to be careful, because when you're work is done, you'll leave, and that will crush me."

Kate closed her open mouth and stuttered out her next words. "It's my job, Chase, my dream. I have to leave."

"I get it. Especially now that I know what you've gone through to get here. I would never stand in your way." He pulled back his arm. "I've made a decision. I don't want you to work for me anymore."

Kate let out a gasp of air. "You don't?"

"No," Chase said, "I want to work with you. I want us to work together."

Kate blinked up at him. "What do you mean?"

"I know the timing of our…*relationship,* is weird. I get it. We both have a lot on the line. We both need the next two weeks to go perfectly." He smiled. "We have the same objective, Kate. I just want us to work together from now on. No more secrets. Just mutual respect."

He saw her soften. "That's it?" she asked.

"That's it. From now on, we work together."

She nodded. "I'd like that."

"Good. I hope that also means you're okay if we spend some time together outside of work. It might end, but it doesn't have to end yet."

He felt Kate tighten up.

"No one has to know unless you want them to," he continued. "That's all up to you."

The calculus ran through Kate's eyes. After a

moment, she looked up at him and nodded. "I'd like that, too," she said, and reached her hand around the back of his neck pulling him in for a kiss.

Chapter 19: Kate

Kate hit dial and Lindsey's face popped into view, tiny wet curls dripping from the side of her head. "How's it going? I've been so nervous for you." she said, grabbing a towel and pinching the ends of her hair.

Kate reached out and touched the screen. "I'm good. Everything's good," she said. "Thank you for being there."

Lindsey beamed into the camera. "Always."

Kate took a breath and launched into her rundown of the previous week. By the time she was done, Lindsey's hair had dried in perfect ringlets around her pixie face. "Wow, Pipes," she said. "So…let me get this straight. Chase basically outted you. He found out everything and you're okay with that?"

"Yeah, I guess."

"Weird."

"I mean, yeah, I actually feel kind of relieved." Kate shrugged. When she thought about her past, it felt like a terrifying abyss pulling her down, but when Chase talked about it, it all didn't sound like that big of a deal anymore.

"Wow," Lindsey replied. "That's great. So, what next?"

"I've been trying to work that out," said Kate. "It's been a crazy ride, so far."

"True, that."

"The good news is, the crash didn't really hurt us, and the announcement of the IPO has been well received. I've been getting rounds of questions from financial news outlets, as expected, but no interest from any tabloid outlets. All in all, it seems like it might work out." As Kate said that, she felt the skin on the back of her arms tighten and tiny hairs raise all over her body. It seemed like things were going almost too well. *Good stuff happens, too, Kate,* she told herself.

"And with Chase?" Lindsey asked. "Do you think things might work out there, too?"

Kate tried to smile into the camera, but could see on the screen that her face wore more of a frown. "That's complicated. He likes me, and admittedly, I like him. But if this launch goes well—and it will, I'll make sure of it," she said with a slow, determined voice, "I'll be leaving to come back to Boston. Pick up new clients."

Lindsey leaned into the camera. "You know, Pipes, it doesn't have to be all or nothing. They do have these crazy new machines called airplanes."

"I know. That's just too much to think about now. What did you find out about the photographer at the crash?" she asked, changing the subject.

Lindsey typed something into her keyboard and looked at her screen. "A local guy got the credit. I called him, but he wouldn't say much other than that he was hired to be there. When he figured out I was digging, he clammed up."

"That's interesting."

"Isn't it? And I noticed Ms. Oklahoma was wearing a VIP pass in the photo so I did a little research there. Turns out, she wasn't just a spectator and she wasn't at the hospital. She jumped into the photo in the back hallways of the track when Chase was being wheeled out."

"Chase didn't know she was there. Who else would have gotten her a pass?"

"That remains a mystery. She's not a race-hound. She never posted anything from a track, and believe me, that woman posts a lot of pictures of herself."

"Huh. Okay, Lindz. Thanks, gotta run. Company barbecue today."

"Ooh! Fun. Have a hot dog for me."

Kate smiled. "Will do."

Outside, she could hear the clang of picnic tables and umbrellas being set up. She walked to the window and peaked outside. Bo and Big Cal were setting up a row of grills on the far side of the lawn, and Peggy, Constance, and Rose were laying red plaid tablecloths across the tables. Kate looked from side to side with a slight frown. No Chase. She checked herself once in the mirror, hoping the simple sun dress she wore would be alright, then stepped outside.

"Hi there," she said to Rose. "Can I help?"

"Kate!" Rose said as a smile spread across her face. She rushed over to Kate and grabbed her. Rose hugged her so tightly that Kate wondered how Rose stayed in such good shape at her age. Rose held Kate by the arms as she withdrew slightly to look her in the eye. "You are a gem," Rose said.

"I am?"

"I think Cal bringing you here was one of the smartest things he's ever done." Rose nodded. "The way you've handled everything has been top notch. And, the way you've worked with Chase," she leaned in, "you make a good pair. A little like me and Cal, I'd say." Rose let go and ended the hug with a little wink.

Kate blushed. "Um, thank you."

"Peggy," Rose called out. "Get over here and give Kate a hug."

Kate looked across the lawn at Peggy, who

lifted her head with a scowl. "I'm fine over here, Rose."

"Don't give Peggy a second thought," Rose whispered. "She'll come around."

Kate nodded and walked out from the shade of the porch into the warmth of the mid-day sun, stretching her arms above her.

"Hi there," she heard Chase say, and turned to see him beaming at her.

"Hello," she smiled in return.

"Would you like to grab a table with me?"

"Sure."

Chase took her by the hand and led her to a table shaded by a giant poplar tree. Kate looked around, but no one seemed to care that she and Chase were holding hands. She exhaled and squeezed his hand as they sat down.

The lawn filled with employees as the afternoon went on, and she and Chase watched from the side as people made their way back and forth to the grill. Cal wore an apron that read "Don't Cook Bacon Naked", and lifted burgers on and off of the grill and onto plates with a smile and a laugh. Every once in a while, Rose would come over and give him a cool beer and a kiss on the cheek before retreating back to her table.

Kids ran around the lawn screaming in glee as they tried to spray each other with bubble guns. Tommy popped up everywhere with his camera, laying on the ground or standing on a chair, trying to get the best shot.

The sun filtered down through the leaves of the trees which danced with the growing breeze. Kate took a deep breath and closed her eyes. She and her sister used to run through grass just like this when she was a kid. And her parents would hold her and tell her she was special and that they loved her. Behind her closed eyes she felt tears rising. *Have I forgotten what's really important?* she asked herself.

She felt Chase put his hand on her thigh, and with her eyes still closed, she reached down and put her hand over his. She could feel him looking at her. She turned towards him, opening her eyes. He looked at her with his dazzling green eyes and she expected to see another smile, but this time, she saw him looking at her like a ripe apple he wanted to peel. Blood rushed up her neck.

"I think the launch went well," she said.

Chase looked at her steadily. "Uh huh," he said.

"The major outlets picked up the safety test spin, so I think we're good there."

He tilted his head and stared at her. "Can't we take one day where we don't talk about work?"

Kate pulled back and looked him in the eye. "No. We only have two weeks left. Every day counts."

"Exactly," Chase said. "*We* only have two weeks left. I'd like to just spend some time with you. Why can't it just be easy?"

"If you wanted easy, you should have gone for Ms. Oklahoma," Kate said with a grin.

Chase made a face. "She's not my type."

"Right, because blond and beautiful is so icky," Kate deadpanned.

"Not all men are into that."

"They're not?" Kate said, dubious.

Chase looked down at her, amused. "My type seems to be bossy and emotionally unavailable."

Kate glared at him. "You don't know me that well."

Chase clutched her hand again. "Well, I know you like dance parties in your kitchen. You twirl your hair when you're nervous. You hate to drive fast. You like barbecue. You're intelligent and loyal. And your Boston accent comes out when you drink."

Kate shot him a dirty look. "It does not."

"Yeah. Kate Piper turns into Kate Pie-Puh. It's cute."

Kate flushed red. "I thought I had gotten rid of that."

Chase continued. "As far as I'm concerned, you're perfect."

"Oh, please," Kate rolled her eyes. "I'm not perfect."

"You are for me."

As he looked at her, Kate felt like the only other person at the barbecue. She was suddenly aware of his arms and thighs next to her, emotion vibrating off of him. He leaned toward her, his eyes fixated on her lips then back on her eyes. She did not break his gaze, and as they looked at each other, she felt heat rise up at the base of her neck, in her belly, and between her legs.

"I think this is the most time we've spent together since the hotel," Chase said, his voice low.

All Kate could manage to do in response was nod. She suddenly wanted to touch him, to feel the length of his skin against hers. She had just begun to close the gap when a gust of cold wind swirled around them. Chase looked up.

"Storm's coming in," he said.

Dark rolling clouds tumbled over the sky, and the breeze brought with it tiny cold flecks of rain.

"Does it always change so quickly here?" Kate asked.

"This is Oklahoma. You never know."

"Everybody grab something," Rose called out, and people that remained at the barbecue started grabbing dishes and plates and running into the nearest doors as the rain began to land in thick, fat drops.

"Chase," Rose yelled, raising her hand up to her mouth to be heard, "Get my tablecloths!"

Chase hopped up, his hair being blown one direction then the other. "Get inside," he yelled over the wind.

"No, I'll help," Kate replied.

Together they ran from table to table, piling the wet table cloths in their arms, then running for Rose's front door. By the time they got inside, they were both wet and gasping.

Rose followed them in with a stack of dishes. "You two put those in for a quick wash, please."

Kate followed Chase to the laundry room at the back of the house. They packed the wet tablecloths into the washer and hit the on button.

"I'm soaked," Kate said, flinging water from her arms.

Chase eyed the wet sundress that clung to her in all the right places. She recognized the look in his eyes. Her eyes widened as she sensed what was coming next. He ran his hands through his hair once then came toward her. He grabbed her hips, pushing her back against the oscillating washer. His eyes slipped down her torso, taking in the tips of her breasts, erect and pushing up through the thin, wet fabric. Then in a rush, his head dropped down and he kissed her neck, his lips and tongue grazing softly against her skin.

His hair smelled like mint or jasmine and Kate breathed it in, the scent of him quickening her pulse like an aphrodisiac. She arched her neck, further exposing it to his hot kisses. She wanted to say something, but the words wouldn't come. Instead, she pressed her hips into him, joining him in a rhythmic sway of need and desire.

Without warning, Chase's mouth was on hers, his tongue sliding in to touch her tongue. She felt another wave of desire as he pushed his knee between her legs, parting them. His hand reached up to her breast, squeezing it softly as he kissed her and pressed his knee up against her.

Kate could hear Rose in the kitchen, putting the dishes away and talking in muffled tones to Big Cal. "Chase," she whispered in a raspy voice. "You're parents are right outside."

"Uh huh."

Kate arched her back, pressing her sex down onto him. Her mind told her to stop, but her body wanted to give itself up to him completely.

"Shouldn't we…" she groaned, "stop?"

Chase took one hand and clutched her knee, then slid his hand up to her inner thigh, his fingers grazing against her.

"Are you sure you want me to stop?" he whispered in her ear as his fingers slid inside of her. "It doesn't feel like you want me to stop."

She couldn't say a word. Her whole body was focused on his fingers, sliding around her clit, then inside of her, then sliding back out to stroke her between her slippery folds. She felt her blood rising as another moan escaped her lips, this time loudly. Chase took his other hand and cupped her around the throat, and then across her mouth. He was working his fingers in and out of her, and she was grateful he was able to stifle her groans with his other hand.

Her core clutched at his fingers, but her legs were weakening to the point she felt like they were on the verge of failing her. She threw her arms around Chase's strong shoulders and neck for support. His muscles tensed as his head bent down, his eyes watching as she unraveled before him, his hand glistening and wet. He held her body up as he kneaded her over and over until she felt herself clench around him and her body flush with release.

Kate leaned against the dryer trying to slow her breathing. Chase held her by the waist and nuzzled into her neck. "My God, you feel good." he said. Kate could feel the rod of his erection pressing through his pants and she reached down, grasping it. He moaned into her neck.

"Chase?" they heard Rose call out. "Is that load done? We have more to wash."

Kate felt Chase swallow. "Almost done," he replied through the door.

They fell together, their arms wrapped around each other, giggling.

"I need a minute before I go out there," he said sheepishly.

Kate held his face in her hands and kissed him long and slow. They did only have two weeks, and Kate was starting to hope they could spend it together.

Chapter 20: Chase

Chase bounded into KinCo Headquarters the next morning. He waved at the security guard downstairs as he walked in. "Good morning," he called out.

"Morning, Chase," the guard said in return. "Beautiful day."

Chase beamed. "It is." He said, then took the stairs two at a time up to the Executive Floor. As usual, on a Monday morning, workers were gathering around, chatting casually about their weekends and getting coffee. The morning light filtered in through the overhead skylights, and Chase felt a renewed sense that all was right with the world. The launch was going well, in two weeks the company would be his, and then there was Kate. Wonderful Kate. Chase smiled. She was giving him a chance. He could have Kate and the company. It was going to be a great day.

"Good morning!" he called out to a group of employees, who looked back at him with curiosity.

Chase stopped by his office to grab a fresh cup of coffee and some notes for a morning meeting, then headed down the hall to the Executive Conference room. Already seated inside was a group of fifty-two key employees, milling around chatting. When they saw Chase come in, they all took their chairs. Chase stepped up to the front of the room. Two rows back, he saw Constance, to whom he gave a quick nod. He had been looking forward to this day and this speech for weeks.

"Good morning, everyone. Thanks for coming in." Chase opened his hands wide and smiled. "As you know, this is an exciting time for the company. Our profits are up. Our product line is expanding. And in a couple of weeks, our brand will go public, and then international. Your contribution has been key to our success and I'm here to thank you for that."

Chase looked around the room at the familiar faces. Most of them had given years to the company, had relocated out to this area to work for KinCo. He knew their families and their lives. He knew which ones were newly married or had kids in college, or an illness in the family. He paused to savor this moment.

"Each of you has made a special contribution to this company. Without you, KinCo would not be what it is today. You deserve to share in our success. To that end," he said slowly, "each of you will be receiving a packet later today, outlining how you will be receiving additional compensation in the form of stock options."

A collective gasp arose from the employees, and several of them looked at Chase open mouthed, while others turned and high-fived their neighbors. Chase beamed at the group. He saw Constance, clutching her purse with tears in her eyes. He mouthed a silent 'thank you' to her before continuing. "When the company goes public, you can sell your stocks based on market value, or keep them and let them grow. All of this will be explained in the collateral you'll receive this afternoon, but if you have any questions, HR can help you."

Chase heard a ping and one of the employees looked down at his phone, then back up at Chase. Then another. Tablets and phones started vibrating across the room. One employee leaned over and whispered something in another's ear. They both shook their heads and looked at Chase in disbelief.

Chase saw Kate enter suddenly from the back of the room. She scanned the faces of the employees and walked briskly to join Chase at the front. "Everybody, thanks, we need to wrap up for now."

"But, Kate," Chase whispered, "I'm not done."

"You totally are, but keep smiling."

Employees stood, some going right for the door, others turning to look at Chase with a question in their eyes. "What's going on?" Chase asked through gritted teeth.

"Just keep smiling."

The employees cleared the room, but many of them lingered outside, watching Chase through the conference room windows. They grouped together, looking down into their phones.

Chase turned to Kate, blood rising in his face. "What is going on?" he demanded.

"Everyone can still see us," she said in a brittle voice. "And never forget they all have cameras in those phones, so keep smiling."

Chase looked dubious. "Okay…" He plastered a smile on his face.

Kate smiled back. "Now, we just look like we're having a pleasant conversation, right?"

Chase nodded.

"Don't blow up," she continued.

Chase's brow furrowed, but he forced the smile to remain.

Kate took a breath and looked up at him. "A tweet went out this morning," she said.

"A tweet?"

"Yes. From your account."

"My account? I haven't tweeted anything in years."

"Someone did." Kate tilted her head and smiled. Her eyes were facing towards him, but she looked as if she was thinking about something else, something sad and far away. "Someone hacked it."

Chase lowered his head.

"Keep smiling," Kate said. "Let me guess. You never closed that account and never changed the password."

Chase gasped and shook his head. "How bad is it?"

"Bad."

Chase felt the room swirl. "Tell me," he said.

Kate clenched her phone, holding it away from her, fingers apart, as if she were touching something horrid. She did not bother to raise the phone up to show him. She cleared her throat as her smile quivered and began to fail. Chase waited for her next words with a sense of dread.

"There is a picture of me in the tweet," she began slowly. "A close up of my cleavage. I was in a chair and bending forward, and let's just say—it was apparently cold when it was taken."

Chase swallowed, then nodded for her to continue.

Kate recalled for him the exact wording of the tweet in a raspy voice, as if she had already read it a hundred times. "It reads: Happy to get my turn with @katepiper working under me. She's looking especially happy to see me today. #itsgoodtobetheboss."

Chase fell back against a desk. "Oh my God." His hand rose to his chest and he loosened his tie.

"They're still watching," Kate said with a strained voice and a thin smile.

"I can't—I don't..." Chase stammered, his shock evident. He looked up suddenly. "Kate," he said, "you know I didn't send that, right? I would never—"

"I know," she interrupted. "Lindsey already figured out the picture was from several years ago when I lived in Boston. My hair was shorter, and the pixels indicate that it was blown up from another photo."

Kate moved just an inch closer. She reached out the tip of her shoe and touched his. He focused on that small touch and tried to ground himself.

"What's the password?" Kate asked softly.

"What?"

"The password for your old account. I'll have Lindsey shut it down."

Chase felt a pain in his chest. He did not want to tell her. "Fitz," he said, shaking his head. "Captain Obvious, I know. How dumb."

He watched as Kate tapped her phone with trembling fingers. It looked like she was struggling to take her next breath. His mind swirled. Of all the things to happen, he had never expected this. His reputation, the IPO, his family. Had he put everything at risk just because he didn't change one password?

Chase gripped the edge of the desk and licked his lips. He felt his eyes and cheeks getting hot. "Are we screwed?" he asked through clenched teeth.

Kate gave a little shake of her head, but her eyes looked unsure. "I don't know. I need to—" she paused. "We need to get out of this room. Go to your office. Get some privacy."

Chase nodded. They exited the conference room, walking upright and nodding assurances to the staff. Kate looked completely in control, but he felt like he was unraveling. He counted the steps until they got safely behind his closed office door. When he turned around, Kate would not look at him.

"Lindsey has closed your account," she said in a clipped voice. "Don't do anything. Don't talk to anyone." She shook her head slightly. "I need to think," she said, then walked out the door.

Chapter 21: Kate

Rain tapped softly against the rooftop as Kate sat in the dark wishing the whole world would just wash away. She had pulled her comforter to the couch and sat there in the dark for hours before daring to look into the cold glow of her tablet. The tweets about her, Chase, and KinCo flew across the globe. She pressed her fist to her lips and choked back a sob. "@KatePiper is a bimbo," read one. "Wear a bra, @KatePiper, you slut," read another. And there were hundreds more. Kate shook her head in wonder and wiped a tear from her cheek.

The tweets about Chase were equally bad. "@ChaseKincaid should be castrated," and "sexists like @ChaseKincaid should never be allowed to run a company." She grimaced at the screen. The financial news had already picked the story up, tying it to the IPO. She tried to focus in on what to do next, but every time she did, she only saw spots in her vision. She found it hard to breathe.

Kate heard the distant chime of a video call in the kitchen. No doubt it was Lindsey calling again. It had been hours since they talked and Kate knew Lindsey was losing her mind with worry, but she couldn't manage talking to anyone, right now. She untangled herself from the comforter and dragged herself to the bathroom to get another box of tissue. *This is it,* she told herself. *This is the end.* Her reputation was shot. Anytime anyone ever did a search of her again, this is what they would find. Kate Piper, joke. Kate Piper, failure.

She shook her head in disgust. They didn't know anything about her. They don't know she had been trying to dig herself out of a deep hole since her family died, that she had been alone and fighting a system that wanted to call her bad and keep her in a box. She had fought her way out, put herself through college, and built a business of her own through sheer determination.

All she ever wanted was to make something of herself. To succeed. Now, that was all taken away. Kate retracted her arms into her torso with a wet tissue clenched in each hand. She felt exhausted.

She couldn't fight anymore.

A soft knocking sound echoed through the house. Kate looked around. It wasn't coming from the front door. She sniffled again and listened. The knock came again, this time from the hallway. Kate padded over and listened. She closed the bathroom door, and behind it, she saw another small door built into the wall. The knock sounded again. Kate hesitated, then reached out and turned the knob.

Chase stood one step down in the open doorway of what must be the stairway to the tornado shelter. Kate remembered vaguely that all the shelters were connected underground. *He didn't want to be seen coming over here,* she thought. *I don't blame him.*

Chase looked up at her from the dark stairwell, a deep line lodged between his eyebrows. He ducked under the door jam and entered the house, silently walking around Kate and into the hallway. He turned and took a deep breath, standing with his legs planted apart as if bracing himself for her anger. She opened her mouth to say something, but no words came.

He looked down at her in confusion. A pained look ran across his beautiful green eyes as she met his gaze and began to sob. She could see the look of surprise in his face, but she couldn't summon the will to stop the tears from falling.

He reached out and put his long arms around

her. He held her tight, pulling her head into his chest and stroking her hair. He smelled like rain and cedar, and she breathed him in as a sob escaped her lips.

"Oh, Kate," he said, and she felt his muscles clench as they tightened around her. He pulled her arms gently around the back of his neck, and lifted her up, sweeping her legs off the ground and into his arms. He carried her down the hallway into the darkened bedroom and reached down with one arm, tossing the bed covers aside.

He gently laid her down, brushing her hair back across the pillow. She closed her eyes, welcoming the cool fabric behind her neck. She heard Chase slip off his shoes, then slide in beside her, pulling the covers up around them. As they faced each other, Chase wrapped his strong arms around her waist and pulled her against him. His hand stroked the back of her neck and hair while he planted little kisses on her cheek and mouth. He murmured gently in her ear as he held her, "Shhh, Kate, it's going to be alright." He kissed her again. "Everything will be okay," he said. "I love you."

There was no energy left to fear his words. No energy to respond. Kate simply sobbed into his shoulder as she wrapped her arms and legs around him, clutching at the fabric of his shirt. She felt warm in his arms as tears slid down her face, soaking her pillow. A long, shaking breath left her lips. She was astonished at herself. She cried so much here. She never used to cry at all.

Kate listened to the steady beat of Chase's heart as they lay entwined under the covers in the darkened, private cave of her bedroom. Their arms stayed wrapped around each other as the remaining daylight faded and the room plunged into total darkness. Kate realized she was holding Chase as fervently as he was holding her. They were hiding together. She let herself fall away into the safety of his arms and his perfect embrace. At least for now, she didn't have to be Kate Piper. She was just Kate, safe in Chase's arms.

She must have drifted off into sleep, for as she awoke, a wave of regret crashed over her. She was so stunned by her own personal crisis she had lost focus on Chase and what he must be feeling. A rush of adrenaline swirled through her chest as a final tear slid down her cheek and onto the still damp pillow. She laced her fingers around the back of Chase's neck and took in the scent of his hair and skin one last time, then slid out of his embrace.

As she repositioned the covers over him, she saw his eyes open in the darkness. His hand reached out and took her by the wrist. "Where are you going?" he whispered.

Kate took his hand and lifted it to her mouth, kissing it, then held it to her cheek. "To work," she said, placing his hand back under the covers.

"To work."

Chapter 22: Chase

Chase awoke in the dim gray light of Kate's bedroom to his phone dinging on the bedside table, notifying him of an unread text message. He untangled his arm and reached out to look at the screen. It was Kate. "Come soon. Wear the dark blue suit, white shirt, solid tie."

He blinked at the words and sat up slowly, reaching to rub a stabbing pain out of one of his shoulders. He looked at the time. 9:37 AM. How could he have slept so late? He felt like he had been drugged. His mind shifted and the words in that awful tweet flooded his mind. He groaned and fell back against the pillow. Peggy and his parents must be losing their minds. He sent them all a quick text. "All okay. Will explain. Coming in." He staggered back through the dark corridors of the tornado shelter, then up into his own house. He showered and dressed quickly, giving Fitz a quick rub on his way out. "Don't look so glum, buddy," he said. "Everything will work out, right?"

As he pulled into the KinCo parking lot, the security guard nodded at him, but then averted his eyes. Chase was grateful for that. He didn't know what to say to anyone. He didn't know how to explain. He walked briskly through the hallways with his head down, questions racing through his mind. When he got to his office, his assistant said quietly, "Kate's in there," then, too, looked away.

Kate stood looking out the window. When she heard him enter, she turned. "Good morning," she said loudly enough for his staff to hear. "Let's get started."

As Chase shut the door, Kate rushed over to him, wrapping her hands around his waist and pressing her forehead into his chest. "You're here," she said.

Chase felt his anxiety start to fade away as he held her. "Yes," he said, stroking her back, "and so are you."

She nodded into his chest, exhaled, and then pulled away.

"I owe you an apology," she said. "Yesterday, when you asked if we were screwed, I should have looked you in the eye and said *no, I've got this*." She grimaced. "But I didn't." She took both of his hands in hers and squeezed them. "I'm sorry I wasn't there for you. That won't happen again."

Chase felt tiny springs uncoiling in his belly. He nodded. "We're in this together, Kate," he said. "So you call it. What's next? Because honestly, I have no idea."

She guided him to a chair then sat and looked at him with her perfect blue eyes. "You are doing an interview."

He blinked. "Who?"

"You."

He shook his head. "You know how I feel about that. I can't—"

"Don't worry, I'll prep you." Kate glanced down at her watch. "We have an hour."

"An hour?" Chase said, then realizing his voice was raised, said again, "An hour? Kate, that's crazy."

She placed her hand on his arm and looked at him reassuringly. "Chase, listen. It's happening. It has to."

His head dropped into his hands. He did not want to look back up. The last time he did an interview, he found himself saddled with a crazy stalker. His head felt like it was being squeezed in on both sides. He'd rather be in another fiery car wreck than do an interview.

Kate spoke in a steady, determined voice. "What we do now will determine how this whole story is reported from now on. We can control this narrative, but if we don't fill that space, the media will. We have to do the interview today."

He looked up at her, his voice catching in his throat. "Control, how?"

Kate eyed him evenly. "No one died here, Chase. This doesn't have to be a major scandal. There was no accounting fraud, spying, violation of safety regulations, none of that. Those are the type of scandals that ruin corporations." She shrugged. "Right now, you just look like a misogynistic asshole."

Chase grumbled and rubbed his face with his hands.

"We can control that," Kate continued.

He let out a haggard laugh. "How, Kate? How could we possibly fix that? Deny it? It was my twitter account, for Christ's sake."

Kate shook her head. "No, we don't deny. We don't apologize, and we definitely don't rationalize. The public and the media will eat you alive if you do that."

"What, then?"

"Have you ever heard of Reputation Capital?"

"No."

"When it comes to corporations, Reputation Capital is as important as any other asset. It's an intangible strength embedded in the company's value."

"Okay. I guess they forgot to teach that part in business school," Chase said snidely.

"Funny. Listen, your personal reputation is not what's important here. If we handle this right, we can repair that, too. But what we need to focus on is the company's reputation and your ability to be CEO."

"Agreed."

"If we rationalize, that does nothing to placate the markets. What the market wants is integrity and bravery. Remember that. Integrity and bravery."

He nodded. "Integrity and bravery. Go on."

"I will give you a list of talking points. Have you ever heard a good politician do an interview? No matter what they're asked, they just stick to the talking points. That's what you'll do."

Chase shook his head. "They won't go for that."

"TV Interviews are edited. They don't have room for the back and forth. That's boring. The producer is only looking for the sound byte. That's what our talking points give them."

"What happens when they ask about the tweet? They will ask. That's the whole point, right?"

Kate shook her head. "That's what gets them in door, but then we switch the pitch. We redirect. When they ask any question related to the tweet, you laugh and say, 'I was as shocked as anyone. That was a joke in poor taste. Apparently, we are getting attention because the launch of our IPO is going so well'. Then you launch into the valuation going up. That the result will be more American jobs. That's it. Deflect. Joke in poor taste. You were surprised. Valuation going up. More American jobs. All investors will hear is valuation going up and more American jobs."

Chase looked at Kate in stunned silence.

She nodded at him in reassurance. "You can do this."

Kate reached over to the desk and grabbed a short stack of note cards. "Here are your talking points. You don't have to remember everything. Just don't get in the weeds, and whatever they ask, your three responses are, Joke, Valuation, Jobs. Got it?"

Chase swallowed. "Will you be there?"

"Yes. Not on camera, but in the back of the room." As she looked at him, her eyes got softer. "Do you need a fluff?"

"A what?" Chase scoffed.

"A fluff." She moved her chair so it was directly in front of his and leaned forward. "You listen to me," she said. "You are Chase Kincaid. You are smart and brave, and have built one of the best companies in the United States."

"Kate…"

"No. You listen. No one can lead KinCo into a

new era better than you. Anyone who thinks they can keep you down is mistaken. You are Chase Kincaid, and they don't know who they're messing with. Got it?"

Chase grinned at her. "Yeah."

"Who are you?"

"Chase Kincaid."

"That's right." Kate leaned forward and tenderly kissed him on the cheek. "Okay, then. You prep. I'm going to check on your lighting."

Chase rubbed the sweat from his palms and took a deep breath. Two months ago, when he visualized this final week, he thought everything would come together, the launch would be celebrated, and the company would be his. Now his IPO was in danger, and in seven days, Kate would be gone. Chase felt a hollow black hole in his stomach as he thought of it. He scowled down at the notes one last time, then walked out of his office. He couldn't help but notice KinCo employees turning away from him as he walked down the halls. Everyone was unsure how to respond. He pulled himself up so his back was straight. He would fix this. He would fix everything.

As he walked into the interview room, a giant light ignited across him, bathing everything in cold, white rays. He raised his hand up to shield his eyes. "Is that really necessary?" he asked.

He saw Kate rush across the room to his side.

"Concentrate on your talking points. Everything here is just a tool for you to convey the message." Kate reassured him with a final squeeze to his arm then stepped back behind the lights.

The reporter approached Chase and introduced herself, then directed him to a chair. He took a deep breath. As he did, he looked through the beams of light to see Kate. She was walking around in the background, stepping gingerly around the trail of black electrical cords that littered the floor. She settled in a spot against the wall, leaning there and gazing at him in silent reassurance.

He returned her gaze and suddenly wished they could go back to this morning when they were huddled in bed together, just the two of them, embracing in the darkness. He silently counted the steps between them. It was only twenty feet to Kate's arms, to Kate's skin. He cast his eyes to the ground. Last night, when he told Kate he loved her, she didn't respond. Instead, she got up and went back to work. If he had one more year, maybe he could make Kate love him back, but he only had seven more days.

Chapter 23: Kate

"You might understand how some of our viewers might question your ethical standards given the recent tweet about Ms. Piper."

Chase revealed a charming smile to the reporter. "I don't blame them. That tweet was a poor joke played by someone who clearly doesn't know Kate." Chase pivoted his eyes just slightly, so they looked beyond the reporter back to where Kate stood. Chase looked at her directly. "Kate is my professional colleague. She is brilliant and beyond reproach. We are lucky to have her on our team." Then he cast his attention back to the reporter. "We continue to move forward, looking ahead to the launch of our IPO next week."

Kate reached her hand back behind her and

steadied herself against the wall. The way Chase was looking at her made her body flush. She wanted to look down to compose herself, but her eyes were planted on Chase's mossy green eyes bathed in the camera's lights.

"Will you be a different leader from your father? How will KinCo be different with you at the helm?" the reporter asked.

"Our entire history has been about innovation and creating the best U.S. made products for our customers. We are committed to continuing that tradition."

"We look forward to seeing what happens," said the reporter. After a moment, the lights turned off and the reporter reached out her hand. "Great interview, thank you," she said as she stood.

Kate walked over and handed her a folder. "You are getting this ahead of the pack," she said. "You have a five hour lead."

"Got it, thanks, Kate." The reporter gathered up her things and walked back to her crew.

Chase loosened his tie as he watched her go. "What was that?" he asked.

Kate took a breath. "Press release. Announcing the new Spring product line."

Chase turned toward Kate with a look of admiration. "The art of a fresh narrative, I take it?" he asked, but Kate couldn't respond. She had to wait for the crew to pack up and exit the room.

She remembered to breathe as they exited, shutting the door behind them.

"Chase," she whispered. "About last night—"

"I know, Kate." He frowned. "I know you don't feel what I feel."

"No, I—"

"I'm alright. I know you have to leave soon, and this," he motioned to the space between them, "can get messy."

Kate took a breath and said what she needed to say. "I can do messy."

Chase gave her a look of confusion. "What do you mean?"

"I mean, we just—" She took another breath then looked up at him. "I don't want to waste any more time. If we only have a week, I want to spend as much of that week with you as I can." As she said it she felt the heat in her body rise. "Will you spend tonight with me?"

She saw desire flash in his eyes, then he shook his head and looked away. "I don't know, Kate. Won't that just make things worse? When you leave?"

Kate nodded. "Probably. I just know I'll regret it for the rest of my life if I don't spend this time with you." Her hands clenched together. "I feel like we've wasted so much time already. I understand if you don't feel the same."

Chase took an audible breath. "Come here," he said.

She had never wanted anyone as much as she wanted Chase. She rushed toward him and threw her arms around his neck, pressing her mouth against his, their lips and tongues crushed together in mutual longing.

She could feel his breath, hot and building, lingering with her own as their lips touched. His arms clutched around her waist, pulling her tightly against him. Her breath became ragged as she felt his erection long and hard against her. She wrapped a leg around him as they pushed against each other, Chase swiveling his hardness into her.

They were abruptly interrupted by his cell phone ringing. Chase pulled away with a gasp. "Dammit," he said, running his hands through his hair.

Kate stood up straight, smoothing her skirt down. She wiped at her mouth and tried to lower her heart rate. She watched as he picked up his cell phone. "One minute," he said to the caller, and pressed the mute button.

Kate walked over and raised herself up on her toes, kissing him softly on the mouth. "Seven tonight," she whispered in his ear, then walked out.

******

Kate took a deep breath and looked at herself in the mirror. Her hair hung in long, curling tendrils which brushed down against the straps of a cream camisole. She turned around slightly and looked at herself from another angle. Below the cami, she wore small, silky cream colored shorts which hung loosely just above the curve of her ass. She frowned, wondering if she should change again. *Stop the nonsense,* she told herself. *He's already seen you naked.*

Mixed in with little quivers of anticipation was a lingering fear that she was doing the wrong thing. She shook out her arms and tried to make the nerves fly away. This morning, curled safely in Chase's warm embrace, she knew what she wanted. He had cared about her when he should have only cared about himself. And, even after chasing her relentlessly for weeks, he did not try to have sex with her. He hadn't even tried to reach under the thick layers of her clothes to touch her last night as she cried. He just held her. She wasn't in charge and she wasn't impressive—she didn't have to be. He was there for her anyway.

Today, at the interview, he was still trying to save her. He could have thrown her under the bus to help himself, but he didn't. And the way he looked at her as he spoke, his eyes boring through the lights, right into her, she could barely wait another minute.

She padded over to the blinds and peaked out. Soft lights shone from within Chase's bungalow but there was no movement inside. She scurried over to the cellar door and put her ear to the wood, checking again to make sure it wasn't locked. She did not hear the tap of underground footsteps, so she walked to the kitchen and poured a glass of wine, took a sip, and gave herself over to the ecstasy of waiting.

She finally heard a tiny knock and the creak of a door. When she turned, Chase was standing there in her hallway, his eyes full of questions only her body could answer. Without a word, she walked over to him and placed both of her hands flat upon his chest and looked up at him. "Hi," she said.

"Hi," he grinned, his arms circling around her waist. He bent down and drew his warm mouth across hers. "You taste like wine," he said.

Kate felt a quiver run through her legs. She took a deep breath and moved her hands down to his hips, steadying herself. "Want some?" she asked.

"No," he said softly.

"No?" Kate looked up into his eyes, feeling her throat constrict as she did.

Chase reached up with his fingers and tucked back a tendril of her hair, then ran his fingers down along her jaw. "What are we doing, Kate?" he asked, his eyes glistening.

Kate felt the ground shift below her. The fear of how she would suffer without him in the months to come crushed in on her. But the fear of not having him right now was even greater. She felt her voice tremble as she looked up at him. "I don't know," she answered. "I just know I want you."

She felt Chase's hands grip into fists around her back and his jaw clench as he closed his eyes. When he opened them, he took half a step back and looked down at her, his gaze trailing from her face, down her shoulders, and her torso. He clutched at her hand with his and then ran that hand up her forearm, slowly, watching intently as her skin rose up and flushed beneath his touch. He ran his fingers along her shoulder, and then with one finger, pulled the strap of her camisole down. She felt shivers run along her skin as he did the same on the other side.

She dropped her arms and let the camisole fall to her waist, then down to the floor. She could feel the skin on her nipples harden and tighten before his eyes. He trailed his fingers from her shoulders, down along the tips of her nipples, then softly traced the curves of her breast before running his hands down the soft skin of her belly.

With both hands, he began to trace pathways along her skin, from her hands, back up her arms, and down her breasts to her belly. She stood still, with her arms dropped to her sides as he created a trail as essential and true as gravity, rivers of his touch that she knew would be permanently and invisibly etched on her skin forever.

Then, he placed his hands on both sides of her belly and pushed her slowly back against the wall. He bent down and kissed her gently on the lips, tasting her once before dropping to his knees before her.

He scanned her skin then dropped his head, her belly flush with his eyes, and rested his forehead against her, his fingers lingering on the waistband of her shorts as he breathed her in.

She felt her back arch as she entwined her fingers in his hair. He pulled her shorts down, and then his mouth was on her, his tongue sliding slowly along the soft skin between her legs.

A burst of liquid rushed through Kate and down to Chase's mouth. Kate couldn't tell if she was saying the words 'yes, yes' out loud or if the words were being released silently in her brain. Her body absorbed his touch. This was necessary —like breathing, or eating. Their bodies were meant to be together like this.

As if Chase could feel her thoughts, he gripped her tightly around the waist and drew her even closer down onto him. He laid one hand on her lower belly, steadying her as she began to shudder, his soft tongue gliding over her most tender parts, feeling instinctively the rhythm of her body.

"How—" Kate licked her lips. "How do you know how to do that?"

Chase lifted his mouth away. “Do what?” he asked and delved back into her.

Kate shuddered. “How…how do you know exactly how to touch me?”

At her words, Chase increased the pressure with his tongue, driving her over the edge. She burst around him, her body quivering against his lips. He stood and cupped her gently with one hand as she quivered, then found her mouth with his own and kissed her deeply.

She could feel his erection straining under his jeans and she reached quickly to undo his belt. A fever ran through her limbs as she undid the button and his zipper, releasing him into her hand. He was so hard, the thickness of his erection now fully released as she slid his pants down around his ankles. She reached up and pulled his tee shirt up his torso and then over his head. She had to feel his skin on her skin. She kissed his chest and his nipples, then trailed her tongue down his belly until she reached the hard length of him, so smooth and perfect under the stroke of her tongue.

Chase pulled her back up and grabbed her by the hand, pulling her back to the bedroom. He pushed her down on the bed, then plunged in on top of her, the full length of his body on hers, the skin of his torso finally touching hers. Kate groaned. He pulled both of her hands up over her head so her breasts were straining upwards and exposed. He flicked the top of her nipples with his tongue as he parted her legs with his other hand. She could feel how wet his hand was when he drew it away from her. She arched her back and drew her legs even farther apart, revealing herself totally to him. This is what she needed. This is where she belonged.

Chase pivoted over onto one hip and looked down at her, his body bathed in rays of light cast through the bedroom door. "You are so beautiful, Kate," he said in a whisper, taking her in.

She watched as his eyes trailed over her, looking at her with a hunger she had never seen before. He bent forward and kissed her again, deep and wet, his tongue finding hers as he rolled above her, the tip of his erection pushing against her soft, tender skin.

"Kate," he said simply, and pushed himself inside of her.

Kate felt herself lengthen and tighten around him, the feeling of him inside her sending waves of pleasure through her body. She curved her back and pushed herself against him, wanting every inch of him. He felt her cue and sank himself so deep, Kate shuddered and threw her arms around his back.

Chase drew out of her, just enough that he could thrust himself back in, and then did it again and again until they were rocking together, their bodies dancing, the friction building between them.

Chase shuddered into Kate's neck as he plunged himself deeper. She drew her legs up around him and clutched at his back as waves of pleasure rushed through her, pulsating against him as he buried himself inside of her. He grew even larger as she clenched around him, her muscles throbbing as waves pulsated through her torso and limbs. She cried out as a final shudder ran through them both, their bodies entwined and panting.

Kate wrapped her arms tightly around his back and held him close. She could feel his heart thumping against her and realized in a sweet affirmation that her heart was beating in time with his. She felt her throat tighten as she began to stroke the smooth skin of his neck and back. She wished she could stay in this moment forever.

Chapter 24: Chase

Chase sat behind his desk, looking at the clock. His calendar looked like a quilt of appointments, highlighted and overlapping, and stretching out for weeks to come, but today, he only had one more to get through before he could get home and see Kate. He shifted in his chair as he remembered how she looked this morning, stretched out across the edge of the bed, spent, her hair wild and tangled against the sheets.

They spent their days at the office, passing with a pleasant nod, or sitting across a conference table surrounded by people who didn't know how much they wanted to reach across and touch each other. But at night, Chase made his way through the patchwork of underground tornado shelters to get to her door, where they nestled in behind the closed curtains of Kate's bungalow, making up for the lost hours.

He awoke this morning, the slow throbbing between his legs confirming there had been hours of love-making, and likely not enough sleep, but then he saw Kate come out of the shower, her body covered only by a towel, her pale skin shining, he felt himself stir again. A glance in the bathroom mirror showed that Kate had seen him watching her. She turned toward him with a smile and dropped her towel to the floor. Her skin glistened as she stood before him, naked in the steamy light of the bath. Without preamble, he went to her, burying his head in her neck and against her skin, taking in the scent of soap and mint, and immediately felt her body respond. He reached down between her legs, feeling the nub of her clit stiffen as he pinched it lightly, then grazed it in a circular motion with his palm.

"Good morning," Kate said with a raspy laugh.

Chase dug his hands into her hips, and with one quick motion, flipped her around, propping her up against the counter. In response, he saw her spread her legs and angle her ass toward him. Without a word, he slammed into her hilt-deep and in the bathroom mirror he could see her face transported by pleasure, her eyes closed, and her mouth open as she cried out in time with his thrusts.

Chase gripped her by the hips, pulled back, then thrust again, watching himself slide in and out of her, watching her skin grip his. A delicious friction grew between them as he pivoted into her, grinding against her in a tight, circular motion.

"Good morning, Kate," he whispered into her ear, and in response, she let out a little moan. She finally let him say her name and he loved it. He groaned and closed his eyes. It took every ounce of strength he had not to explode into her. The fever in his body was gripping him, and the way she spasmed around him told Chase that fever was gripping them both.

He spun Kate back around so she was facing him and lifted her up onto the cold tile of the counter. In response, she wrapped her legs and arms around him, and again, he thrust into her. He grabbed her by the back of the neck, her wet hair trailing over his arms, and kissed her. Her mouth tasted so sweet, and he savored it, savored the connection with every last bit of sanity he had left. His body vibrated, sending waves of unbelievable pleasure through him. He spun on a thread, barely attached to his body, riding endless waves of pleasure as he cried out.

Chase felt a stirring in his pants as he remembered. He was glad he was sitting behind a desk.

He looked again at the final appointment on his calendar. Aunt Peggy had insisted on seeing him first thing, telling his staff it was important. *Why did he feel like he was being called to the principal's office?*

Chase took a drink of water and stood, straightening down the front of his pants. All good. He gathered his things and walked to Peggy's office. Along the way, he saw Kate down the hall, but her back was turned and she didn't see him. No doubt, she was working on the conspiracy theory she told him about this morning. While they were having coffee, sore and late, Kate had held him back.

"Chase, I'm worried," she'd said.

"You don't have to worry about me," he responded. "I promise I'll stop asking you to stay." He shrugged. "At least I'll try to stop asking." He reached over and kissed her on the cheek.

"No, it's not that." She walked over to him. "Listen, this is serious," she said, putting her hand on his arm.

Chase put down his coffee and looked at her steadily. "Okay. Hit me."

"Strange things have been happening. Too many things to be coincidence." Her eyes flitted back and forth over his.

His brow furrowed. "Go on…"

"First that crazy guy on the road, then Ms.

Oklahoma being there at the crash, then that stupid tweet." She clenched the side of the counter top, shaking her head. "I can't shake the idea someone is out to get you."

Chase took her hand. "Yeah, but every one of those things you handled. Brilliantly." He shrugged. "And none of those things have affected the IPO or our valuation. If someone wanted to stop our launch, wouldn't they have made a much bigger deal about all of that? Sure, it's crazy that all that stuff happened. And it wasn't fun, that's for sure." He reached out and wrapped his hands around her waist. "But it seems alright now. The launch is in four days and we're still okay."

Kate shook her head. "I don't know. I just can't shake this feeling."

Chase stopped in the hallway as he thought about Kate's worries. He thought of taking a detour and asking her if she'd found out anything else, but Peggy had already spotted him.

"Get in here," she said.

Chase took one last look down the hall toward Kate, but she was gone. He could talk to her later.

"Hello, Peggy," he said, entering her office. "I checked the financials you sent over this morning. Most of it looks good, but I sent section two back to accounting to double check. I think the projections are a bit anemic."

"That's fine," Peggy answered, waving for

Chase to take a chair, "but that's not what I wanted to chat about."

Chase undid his jacket button and sat. "What's up?"

"Kenji Kai and the rest of our banking team have come early."

"What? Why?"

"They're in Tulsa. I can't blame them. All of this PR nonsense has made everybody nervous. I think they just want to keep a closer eye on us for the final few days before the paperwork is signed."

Chase nodded, his brow tight. "Did they say anything else? Any specific concerns?"

"No, but I hear that they are none too pleased with how Kate Piper has handled anything so far.

A laugh escaped Chase's lips. "Let me guess," he deadpanned. "You heard that from Donna Ogrodnick, your new best friend."

Peggy straightened her back and looked down at him from a sour mouth. "I'm not an idiot, Chase. I know everyone has their own agenda…" she set her mouth in a tight line, then continued. "And that includes me."

Chase felt his eyes go wide, but didn't respond.

"You probably don't remember when I was young," Peggy continued, walking around her desk. "But I had dreams, just like you. I wanted to breed horses. Travel." She reached down and wiped an invisible layer of dust from her keyboard. "But KinCo sucked those dreams right out of me."

"Peggy..." Chase started.

"No—" Peggy looked up with sad eyes. "I'm not complaining. I've had a life here, made a contribution. But I only have so many years left, and after this launch, I intend to live that life."

Chase sat back in his chair and looked at her. It was true. She had withered away over the years, and no joy remained in the slack lines of her face. He tried to think back to a time that she was different, but he couldn't. He just remembered brittle Aunt Peggy going to work then back home to her bungalow, alone. No husband, no children, no friends. Chase felt his heart lurch. That could very easily be him in thirty years.

"Peggy," Chase said. "Whatever you want, whatever it is, I will support you."

Peggy tried to smile, but that didn't come easy. "I know you will if you can, Chase, but that's why I have to know this IPO is going forward. That money means I can finally get out of here."

Chase was stunned. How could he have missed how unhappy Peggy had been all these years? "Peggy, we could have hired someone to replace you years ago, if that's what you wanted. We would never hold you back."

She scoffed. "Well, you say that, and I know you mean it, Chase, but I tried. For years, I tried, but one thing after another always seem to pop up, and after a while, I just gave up. This IPO is my chance. It can't be screwed up."

"It won't be."

"Yeah? Well Donna says Kai is nervous." She looked Chase right in the eye. "Tell me right now, Chase…is there anything to be nervous about?"

Chase thought back to this morning and Kate's concerns something bad was looming, but looked across at Peggy's eyes, imploring him to let her go. He shook his head. "No, Peggy," he said. "Everything is great."

As he smiled and reassured her, he had a wave of panic come over him. He had to find Kate.

Chapter 25: Kate

"Did you get it?" Kate asked into the camera.

"Yup," answered Lindsey, swiveling around in her chair. "I got her cell." Lindsey read the number. "I thought Ms. Oklahoma was old news."

"Just a hunch."

"Well, your Kung-Fu is strong. I no longer question."

Kate gripped her hands together. "Lindz, listen, something else has happened."

Lindsey turned away from one of her many screens and stared into the monitor. "Yeah?"

Kate nodded and a smile stretched across her face. "I got a call from Lou Tarly."

"Lou Tarly, the Estate Attorney? The one who

referred you to KinCo?"

"The very same. So...," Kate hesitated, then shook it off. "He called to tell me that he has been very pleased to see how we handled the various *issues* that have popped up here."

"Uh huh."

"And that he and a group of other well-established Boston attorneys and Family Offices want to keep us on retainer. An exclusive, three year retainer." She beamed into the camera. "We're saved."

Lindsey jumped out of her chair, hitting her knee against the desk. "Sugar dumplings!" she yelled out, rubbing her knee. "Kate! That's great. Oh my God! That's...that's everything you've wanted."

Kate read the names of her new employers and how much each were contributing to her retainer. She watched as Lindsey's mouth dropped open, wider by the second. The variety of clients and assets were amazing. Any one of them would be a dream to work for, and now, she would get to work with all of them. It was beyond anything she had dreamed.

She searched her mind for a happier feeling, then chastised herself for not finding it. It was exciting, yes. But it wasn't enough. *Can't you ever be happy, Kate?* she asked herself, then shrugged into the camera. "So, that's happened." She tried to gin up her voice. "Yay."

Lindsey scowled into the camera. "Hold up. You're not happy. How could you not be happy? I'm confused."

Kate felt tears pool in her eyes. "Sure, I'm happy. Back to Boston with a boat-load of A-list clients to handle? Sure. It's good."

"But..."

Kate frowned at Lindsey. "But, I guess I'll miss Chase."

"Hmm. Why can't you still see Chase *and* take this new job?"

"Because," Kate squeaked. "Everyone will know. And they'll think I bang my clients." She slumped down in her chair. "Plus, I'm sure he'll be really busy. And so will I! And it's just too hard."

"Wow, Kate," Lindsey said. "When has something being hard ever stopped you? You're Kate Freaking Piper, after all." When Kate didn't respond, she continued. "What did Chase say?"

"I haven't told him, yet. He should be here any minute." Kate looked at the clock. "The weather is awful, he must have been held up."

"Good luck, Pipes. I'm sure things will work out," Lindsey smiled reassuringly into the screen. "You know I'm here if you need to talk. Bat things around."

"I know. For now, let's just focus on the launch. Get that call done for me."

"You got it, boss."

"Thanks, L—," she began to say, but the screen went black, along with all the lights in the house.

"Holy shit," Kate muttered to herself. It was still late afternoon, but the sky outside had almost blackened. She pulled out her phone and hit the screen to illuminate the room. Across the way she could see the power had been knocked out in all the houses in the compound.

Rain battered the roof, and every few moments, lightning would flash through the windows followed by the crash of thunder. Kate shuffled over to the hall closet and looked inside. After rummaging around, she found a box of candles and matches. She lit several and put them in the kitchen, then wrapped herself up in a blanket and waited on the couch for Chase.

She had to leave sometime, they both knew that. In four days, the IPO would be launched and she would have to get on a plane back to Boston and to her new job. She tried to feel excited, but felt a surge of fear, instead. She didn't want to hurt Chase, but she knew this would crush him. After the launch, he'd be incredibly busy. He'd meet lots of new people, and he'd move on, she told herself.

She wrapped herself more tightly in the blanket and gave an audible sigh. She didn't think she would move on, but she'd have her work, and that was always everything she'd wanted. *Wasn't it?*

With a rattle, Kate heard the cellar door open. "Kate?"

"In here!" she called out.

Chase emerged into the candlelight with Fitz tucked under one arm, a bouquet of red roses in a vase in the other. "He's afraid of lightening," Chase said as he walked into the living room. He pulled another blanket off the back of the couch and held it up for Fitz. "Come here, boy," he said. Fitz walked over with his head hung, his tail tucked between his legs, and got under the covers. "Good boy," Chase said, wrapping the blanket around him. Fitz nuzzled Chase's hand and gave a low whimper.

Chase turned to Kate and handed her the roses. "Some storm, huh?"

"Thank you," she said as she nodded. She inhaled the heady scent of the flowers, then placed them on a nearby table. How could she ever break his heart when he was this sweet?

Chase came over and kissed her softly on the mouth. "What's the matter, baby? You scared of thunder, too?"

"Nope. I just need to talk to you."

"Yeah? Me, too." Chase said, lifting up the blanket and curling in beside her. "I've been anxious to get here all day."

Kate smiled. "You have?"

Chase wrapped his arm around her. "Yeah, I

had the strangest meeting with Peggy today."

Kate felt her anxiety wain. She had a moment before she had to tell him. "What about?"

"I don't know how I didn't see it," Chase began. "I mean, I never thought she was a happy person, but I thought that was just her modus-operandi, you know?"

"Uh huh."

"Turns out, she's miserable. Has been for thirty years."

"No kidding?" Kate sniffled, hoping Chase hadn't heard her.

He hadn't. He turned to her and took her by the hand. "Kate, I've been thinking. No joking around, now," he said. "I don't want you to go back to Boston."

Kate felt a stab in her chest. "What?" she muttered, shaking her head. "You can't be serious."

"As a heart attack. I want you here. With me."

Kate tried to pull away, but Chase pulled her close, then reached up and took her face softly in his hands, his eyes wet in the soft glow of the candlelight. "Kate, I love you," he said and then he kissed her, his lips softly caressing hers. She felt herself soften and the words "I love you, too," rang through her head, but did not come out of her mouth. Instead, she pulled away. "Chase, I can't. I—"

Thunder crashed against the sky outside,

lighting up the room for a second before a tumult of hail began to hit the top of the house. Kate bolted upright, her eyes wide as she heard the force of the wind make the old wood of the house creak and whine, forcing the glass of the windows to pop back and forth inside of their wooden frames.

Chase rose and clutched her hands, forcing her to look directly at him. "Kate, you can. You can. We can work it out," he yelled over the howling wind outside.

Kate felt tears well up in her eyes and dropped her head, hoping Chase couldn't see.

"Whatever it takes," he continued. "We'll figure it out. I don't want to be without you," he said. "I can't."

The storm shook the house. Kate wanted to say something, anything to make Chase feel better, but she knew her voice wouldn't be heard over the wind. Instead, she reached out and kissed him, hoping he would feel everything she needed to say through her touch.

The house popped again and Kate tore her face from his, her skin rising. She felt her mouth go dry as the walls rumbled along with the furniture they sat on. A siren began to blow in the distance. Chase pulled away and jumped up from the couch. "Storm shelter," he said, reaching out his hand.

Kate froze, looking at the house and her

beautiful roses quivering in a sudden draft that careened through the house.

"Now!" Chase yelled. With a whistle, he called Fitz from the couch, then grabbed the blanket and the box of candles before holding open the cellar door for Kate. The three of them made their way down the dark, steep staircase as the storm thundered overhead. Chase took her hand and led her to a chamber just below what she thought was her bedroom. There was an old, moldy smelling couch in the corner, and she and Fitz curled up on it as Chase lit two candles and put them on the floor. He grabbed the blanket and threw it over the three of them as he sat down. He curled his arms around her and patted Fitz on the back.

"Was that a tornado warning?" Kate asked in a hushed voice as she stared wide-eyed at the ceiling.

"Yup," Chase said cavalierly, "happens all the time here. No big deal."

Kate looked at his eyes in the light of the candles and could see lines furrowing his brow. He curled his arms tightly around her, his muscles clenched.

Kate tried to sound cheerful. "Good," she lied. "I like a good adventure."

Even below the house, they could hear the wind and lightening tear through the sky above them. A crack of lightening hit somewhere close, and Kate wondered what would happen to them if the house above them caught on fire. She curled up tightly in Chase's arms and concentrated on the soothing sound of his breath instead of her own heart which pounded in her ears.

The siren continued, but for a moment, the air above them quieted. She raised her head, hoping it was over, but then, there was a deafening crack, and something like a train bore down on them, shaking the earth.

Debris and dust began to fall from the rafters above. Chase covered Kate's head with his arms as the foundation shuddered around them, scattering loose pieces of wood and brick to the ground around them. It sounded like the world above them was being blown away. Kate clung to Chase, praying they weren't blown away with it.

The support beams of the cellar cracked and swayed around them, bending toward them as if in a nightmare. Kate heard her own scream mix with another deafening crash, and then... nothing. She clutched at Chase, breathing in waves of dirt with her eyes closed, and waited. The world above them had gone totally silent. She raised her head and looked around. One of the candles had blown out, but in the dim light of the other, she saw dust flying around the room and a single ray of light shining through a crack above them.

Chase gave her a sudden squeeze and a hard

kiss on the mouth. "We're okay," he said, squeezing her again, holding her hair in his hands.

Still a bit stunned, Kate merely nodded.

They stood on shaky limbs, and holding onto each other's arms, made their way over a fresh trail of bricks and debris to the cellar stairs. They clawed their way up, pulling pieces of wood out of their way and tossing them aside with a crash. Finally, the cellar door was visible in the rubble. Chase drove his shoulder into it, splinters of woods flew around them as the door opened. As dust settled, they emerged together into what was Kate's hallway, but the roof of the house was gone.

Chapter 26: Chase

Chase could barely feel Kate's fingernails digging deep into his arm. "Oh my God," she whispered.

It took a moment for him to reconcile what he was seeing. He and Kate stood side by side, surrounded by bright pink pillows of insulation which billowed around their ankles, floating across shards of splintered wood and brick that splattered across the ground in what had been Kate's bungalow. Chase blinked rapidly, then focused on a door jamb that was left standing. He grabbed Kate's hand roughly, and together, they staggered toward it, grabbing the door knob which leaned backwards into his hand as he touched it. As Chase pulled, the hinges fell off and landed on the floor with a thud. He blinked again, then lifted the door off the ground and leaned it against a side beam.

Outside, the trees were stripped like barbecue skewers stuck haphazardly in the ground, bare of leaves and branches. Pieces of earth had been lifted and turned upside down, revealing roots that had once been planted far in the ground. All that was green was now brown. Torn earth and wood littered the compound. A silence hung unbidden in the air as if the world watched in hushed tones at the destruction.

Chase put his hand to his chest as he looked down the row of houses. Each had its own individual injury, some missing sections of roof or walls, like flesh pulled from the sides of the houses. He stumbled down the steps of Kate's bungalow and squinted far down the street. He tried to remember which door was his, and who lived in the next one, and the one after that, but his mind fell flat.

Fitz bounded past him across what was once the lawn toward their old front door, whimpered in confusion, then turned to look at Chase in expectation. "Come, Fitz," was all he could manage to say. He closed his eyes and reached out for Kate, pulling her close, holding tightly onto her waist.

"We're okay," he heard her say as she held him close. "We're fine."

Her voice rang clear in his mind and he nodded. They were alive. He held her into his chest crushing her as close as he dared, murmuring a silent prayer of thanks up into the now clearing sky.

"Kate," he said. "I—I don't know what I would have done if…"

"I know," she wrapped her arms around him. "I know."

He turned to her, his eyes burning. "No, you don't," he said, gripping her tight. "I need you. None of this makes sense without you."

Kate nodded up at him. "I'm here." Chase looked at her in awe. Her hair was covered in dust, tear stained streaks lined her face, everything as far as they could see was destroyed, and still she remained strong. *How did this amazing woman come into my life?* he wondered. He reached for her again and wrapped his arms around her. When this was all over, he was going to marry Kate, even if it took a hundred years for her to say yes.

Out of the corner of his eye he saw movement. "Mom…" he murmured, then let Kate go and sprinted down the street.

Rose was coming around the corner of her house, covered in a white powder Chase could only assume it was plaster. She turned and pulled Cal along beside her.

Chase rushed to her side and felt Kate run up

beside him.

"Mom! Are you alright?" Chase yelled as they approached. "Dad?"

As Chase took the weight of Cal into his arms, Rose took a deep breath and released a ragged cough. Kate rushed to wipe the powder from Rose's face and arms, her eyes scanning Rose for injuries. Cal had a gash in his forehead where something had struck him. Chase pulled him over to what remained of their front porch and sat him down.

"Are you alright?" Chase asked, running his hands over Cal's arms and torso. "Are you hurt anywhere else?"

"Fine," Cal wheezed. "Fine, Son."

The four of them sat together on the steps and took a collective breath as they looked around.

Rose spoke first. "House did pretty good there for a while," she began, "but then something gave and stuff just started falling on us."

"Lit us up like a rigged slot machine," Cal said.

"Luckily, we made it down to the shelter." Rose added.

Chase hung his head. When he was a kid, those shelters were a place to hide. He never thought they'd really save everyone he loved.

"We need to check on the others," Cal said, pushing himself up off the ground.

"No," admonished Chase, holding up his

hand. "You stay and catch your breath. I'll go."

Chase stood and looked again down the row of houses. He saw doors begin to open up, or people crawl out of holes that once were walls. Peggy emerged from her house with a look of relief and came toward them, grabbing Chase and holding him tightly. "You're okay," she gasped. "Thank God." Then she stumbled over toward Rose and Cal, hugging them both as she plopped down onto the ground beside them.

A moment later, Sallie and Bo emerged, Sallie pulling her two oldest by the hand to the clearing, Bo carrying the baby in his carrier, and shielding everyone under his thick arms as if something would still fly out of the sky and land on them.

When Chase saw Bo, he ran over and pulled him into a hug.

Chase looked them over and saw they all had small scrapes and were covered with dust, but were otherwise unharmed.

"Whatcha got there?" Chase asked Tommy.

Tommy looked down into his own arms and then pulled the contents close. "My stuff," he said softly, tears coming unbidden to his eyes.

"He would not get down to the shelter without his camera and devices," Sallie said, grabbing Tommy roughly around the neck and planting a kiss on the side of the head. "Nearly killed me with panic."

Tommy looked up at her as a tear washed

down his dirty cheek. "Sorry, Mom."

Sallie wiped his cheeks and then her own "Stop that. I'm just happy you're alright." She looked around with wide, sad eyes. "That we all are."

Chase took a long look around the clearing, watching families emerge with their children and pets, happy again they had those shelters. He wasn't sure everyone else in town would be as lucky.

"Bo, come with me. We need to go door to door."

"Yup," Bo said in response.

Chase turned to Kate and grabbed her hand. "There'll be a shelter set up at the school. That's what the town planned for. You go with Sallie, I'll meet you there."

Kate looked up at him, nodding as fresh tears fell from her eyes. She started to say something, but then shook her head. "Okay," she whispered then pulled his head forward, kissing him hard on the lips.

They embraced and Chase breathed in, once again grateful that Kate was safe.

"Oh, and take Fitz, will you?"

Kate nodded and squeezed his hand.

He watched as Kate and Sallie gathered up the kids and other neighbors, pouring them into running cars and heading down the littered street toward the school.

"Let's roll," he said to Bo. As they approached the first house, Chase tried to remember who lived there. Funny how he knew his neighbors by what color flowers they kept in the front yard, or their front mat. Now all the houses looked the same. Chase pounded on the front door before Bo came over and smashed it open with his shoulder. The house shuddered a bit and a thin, gray cat bolted outside. Satisfied there was no one else, they went on to the next house.

When they had gone through all twenty houses in the compound, the remaining residents sat winded and forlorn, scattered on the clear patches of ground. Chase went back to Cal, Rose, and Peggy, bringing them some blankets and bottled water he saved from his garage.

"Hell of a thing," Rose said, and the rest just nodded, too exhausted to speak.

Chase jumped to his feet at the sound of distant buzzing, scared that the twister had come back. The wind kicked up around him and he covered his eyes as a helicopter softly landed in a nearby field. He blinked in confusion. The blades whirred to a shudder, then a stop, and out of the cockpit hopped Kenji Kai. He strode over to Chase and reached out his hand. Chase took it in confusion.

"We flew over KinCo," Kai said sternly. "Much of it is gone. Your plant, your warehouses."

Chase felt the world drop out below him.

"We need to go now," said Kai. "No time to waste."

Chase was stunned. "You still want to go forward?"

"Perhaps," said Kai. "We need to negotiate. No time to waste."

Rose, Cal, and Peggy walked up beside them. Kai continued. "Roads are out. All gone. We take chopper," he said, motioning toward the helicopter. Chase looked beyond the rubble, then back at his family. He thought of Kate, safely at the school with Fitz. He slowly nodded his head.

"Alright, Kai. Let's go."

Chapter 27: Kate

Covered in debris, townspeople stumbled into the high school auditorium. Kate watched as one man stumbled through the door, then looked around in a daze, turning in circles. He kept reaching his fingers gingerly up to his battered scalp as his lips quivered and moved. Kate walked slowly up to his side.

"Can I help you?" she asked.

The man turned his weary eyes on her as if trying to place her face. "The pot," he said. "I left the pot on the stove." He pulled his fingers away from his scalp, looking down at his darkened fingertips in confusion. "I have to get the pot," he said.

A young woman came up beside him, linking her arm through his. "The pot is gone, Dad," she said. “Everything is.” She gave a nod to Kate, then led the man away.

Kate returned to Sallie, helping her fold out emergency cots, then sat on one, her shoulders slumping. She glanced at the door again and watched as volunteers took names and handed out water. At this rate, they would run out of supplies soon. Chase had still not come through the door.

A man in a checked shirt and old baseball hat entered and walked to the front desk. Kate saw as someone motioned toward her. The man walked up and nodded. “Ma'am,” he said. “Are you Kate Piper?”

“Yes. What’s happened?” she asked, jumping up. “Is it Chase?”

“I don’t know, Ma’am. All I know is some lady, a very persuasive lady, told me I had to drive over here in my truck and let you talk to her on my CB.”

Kate blinked up at him confused.

“She’s out there, on the CB, waiting,” he said. “If you wouldn’t mind…I’d like to get home to my own family.”

“Of course,” she said. “Lead the way.”

The man led her out to a dented semi that idled unsteadily on the uneven road. Kate lifted herself up into the cab. The driver reached over her and pointed. “That’s it right there,” he said. “Just pick it up and hit the side button.”

Kate reached in and did as he said. "Hello?" she said.

"You should say 'over'," came back Lindsey's voice.

"What? Lindsey? How did you find me here?"

"Wasn't easy. Cell towers are out. Phones are out. Internet is out. What a mess. Then, just when I thought there was no way to reach you, I thought of CBs. That's how I found Dan."

"Dan?"

"The trucker. You okay, Pipes?"

"Yes, thank God. Chase and I had a tornado shelter. We were lucky. Some of the other people here," she said as she shook her head, "maybe not so much."

There was a pause. "Listen, Pipes, I hate to pile on, but I think we've got a big, big problem."

Kate felt the blood drain from her face. "What?"

"Well, when I was doing research on Ms. Oklahoma and that photographer, I thought I'd go back to the Gala and see if he had any credits there, see if I could tie together some of his other work. I stumbled on some photos of Kenji Kai."

"The Investment Banker?"

"Well, that's just it. He's based in Japan, so I had trouble linking him to any social media or companies there. Their Internet can be totally different, so I put that on the back burner and built a couple of filters to try to pull info. Today, I got a hit." Lindsey paused again.

"Just say it, Lindz. What is it?"

"According to what I've found, he hasn't always been an investment banker. In fact, I couldn't find anything saying he was ever an investment banker. He's a corporate raider."

Kate sat up in the cab of the truck and found herself gripping the wheel.

"What?"

"Seems his specialty is buying and dismantling companies and selling them for their parts. He keeps the name, but takes over all their operations."

Kate took a breath. "What about manufacturing, Lindsey? Does he manufacture goods?"

She heard Lindsey typing. "Hold, please." Lindsey said. Then, "Yes, his other companies manufacture goods all over Asia. What are you thinking, Pipes? I hear the wheels turning."

There was a long pause, then Kate gripped the CB. "Is the internet down in Tulsa?"

"No. I don't think the storm went that far."

"Okay. I'm going to send you some stuff. I need you to put something together for me. Fast."

"You got it."

"You're a life saver, Lindsey."

"Shucks, I know. Over."

Kate smiled and hung the CB back in its cradle. She thanked the driver and ran into the gym.

"Sallie! Sallie! Where is Bo?"

"He just got back. What's going on?"

Kate turned and saw him. "Is Chase with you?"

Bo frowned. "He went to KinCo with the family and that Japanese dude. What's wrong?"

"Any of those fast cars still working?"

Bo pulled his hat off his head as he ran his fingers through his hair. "Yup."

"I need you to drive me to Tulsa."

"Hold on, now," she heard Sallie say.

Kate turned to her. "Sallie, I would never ask, except, if I'm right—these people aren't just going to lose their houses. They are going to lose their jobs and this town. I have to get to Tulsa."

Sallie put her hands on her hips. "Bo? What do you think?"

"Chase in trouble?"

"Yes."

"Then, yup. I'll get the car. Meet you out front." He scooped up Sallie, kissing her on the mouth. "Okay, hun?"

She nodded, "You'll get back here soon as you can. I know that."

Bo released Sallie and she watched him walk out the door.

Kate spoke. "Sallie, I know I'm asking a lot. I wouldn't ask if—."

"Stop right there," said Sallie. "Any fool can

see you love Chase. I know what it's like to love a man, Lord knows I do. You go do what you have to do."

Kate felt a rush of gratitude. "Thanks, Sallie."

Kate turned to Tommy, who was sitting on a cot, looking at photos he had taken since the storm. "Hey, Tommy," she said. "How would you like to get your first photo credit?"

She saw Tommy's eyes light up. "What do you mean?"

"I'd like to buy your photos."

"Really?"

"Yup. But I need you to trust me to pick out the ones I need from your stash. Would you let me borrow your flash drives until tomorrow?"

She watched as Tommy clutched at a box sitting beside him, taking her in with a calculated stare. He loosened his grip. "Okay," he said. "But be careful."

Kate reached down beside him and took the box. "I will, I promise."

Kate ran for the door and waited outside for Bo. He came tearing around the corner in a sleek red corvette. Kate opened the passenger door and plunged down into the seat. "It's so close to the ground," she said, reaching back for the seatbelt.

"Yup," replied Bo, turning to her. "Fast, right?" he asked.

"Fast as you can," Kate replied, taking a breath and gripping the side of her seatbelt.

Bo revved the engine twice then peeled out. They flew through the streets towards Tulsa, passing the devastation of the tornado along the way. Emergency vehicles passed them going the opposite way, and as the streets and buildings flew by, Kate tried to align her thoughts.

If her suspicions were correct, KinCo was in major trouble. If she was wrong, her own career would be over. She could lose all her clients in Boston, and her second chance would be over. But Chase was in trouble—she had to help him.

An hour later, she and Bo screeched to a halt in front of the Governor's Mansion. Kate asked Bo to wait outside and rushed into the building. A woman in a dark suit looked her over with wide eyes. Kate realized she must still be covered in dirt, and ran her hands once over her clothes. "Kate Piper for the Governor," she said, straightening her back.

The woman let out an incredulous little laugh. "Ms.—I'm sorry, who are you again?"

"Kate Piper. It's an emergency."

"Look around, Ms. Piper," the lady said, gesturing at the dozens of people running in and out of offices and up the stairs. "I'm not sure if you're aware, but it's a day full of emergencies around here. I can leave the Governor your name."

Kate shook her head. "That won't work," she said. Across the lobby she saw the doors to a large conference room open and just inside, the Governor's head towered above the rest. "Mr. Governor!" Kate called out. "Mr. Governor!"

Kate saw the Governor turn his head. She thought she saw some recognition in his eyes, but then he turned away. Kate rushed to the door. As security grabbed her arm, she called out, "Mr. Governor, your jobs initiative is in trouble!"

The Governor turned back and looked at her with a scowl.

"Kate Piper," Kate said. "We met at your Gala. I'm with KinCo."

The governor put down his paper and walked toward her, waving for the security officers to let go of her arms. "Ms. Piper," the Governor said. "I'm sure we all have our fair share of problems today, but my State is a dumpster fire right now. I'm sure we can get you on the calendar in the coming weeks, but today I cannot help you."

"Mr. Governor, if I don't speak with you right now, I believe," she took in a breath. "I believe you will lose all the KinCo jobs in your state and the jobs you've promised your constituents from the KinCo expansion. If my math is right, that's fifteen percent of the jobs in Oklahoma."

She saw the Governor's eyes grow wide. "You can't be serious."

"I am," said Kate. "And I need your help to stop it. Right now."

Chapter 28: Chase

The Kincaid family huddled in the corner of the conference room under flickering, generated lights. As they'd flown over the decimated remnants of what was their town and their company, Chase was left with a hollow pit in his stomach. The earth from the family compound to company headquarters looked like the curling, decaying remnants of a peeled orange, the ground turned up and dropped in piles everywhere. The buildings around the company were shredded at the edges, but mostly intact. Cal estimated about twenty percent of their manufacturing capacity was gone. Even worse, all the roads going in and out of KinCo were destroyed. They would not be able to get the materials in to rebuild for some time.

"I think we should take the deal," said Peggy.

"I don't know. This is too fast," said Rose. "Cal, what do you think?"

"Well, my daddy always said not to make any major decision from a position of weakness. I don't know about you all, but I'm feeling pretty damned weak, right now."

They all nodded in gritty silence.

"Chase?" asked Rose.

Chase shook his head. "We have a responsibility, here," he said. "What about our employees? If we can't rebuild for a year, what about those jobs?" He clenched his teeth. "If Kai says he can transfer some of that load to his facilities for a year, maybe we should take him up on it."

"And go through with the IPO *now*?" asked Rose.

"You can't blame them for wanting that," Peggy said. "After all, it's that or nothing. They were clear. If they make an investment in our manufacturing and distribution, they want that IPO signed to protect their interests. Makes sense."

Chase looked over at Kai and his team, huddled in the other corner. Donna Ogrodnick gave Chase a stern nod. "I don't know," said Chase. "I'd feel a lot more comfortable if I could run this by Kate, first."

"Kate?" Peggy scoffed. "What the hell for? What does she know about corporate finance? Or IPOs, for that matter? She might know how to ping somebody or twitterpate, or whatever, but this is my area of expertise, let's not forget." She nodded in affirmation. "And I say do it."

"Peggy," Rose said. "Kate has saved our bacon. Don't forget that. We would have been toast if she hadn't been here this last month."

Cal took Chase's arm and pulled him to the side. "Kate's gone."

"What?" Chase asked. "What do you mean *gone*?"

Cal looped his fingers through his pants. "IPO is over, Chase. Her job is done. And she's got that new job waiting for her in Boston."

"What new job?"

"She didn't say? Well, you can't blame her, I guess. Lou Tarly has set up a whole group of new clients for her. Keeping her on retainer. Pretty good gig for Kate, from what I hear."

Chase felt the wind go out of him. He steadied himself against a table. "No, she didn't tell me."

"Look, Son," Cal said, placing a beefy hand on Chase's shoulder. "I'm not a blind man. Or an idiot. I can see you've got feelings for that girl. But you'll have to deal with that later. Listen, this is your moment. This is your time to take over the company and make it your own, sad as it is." Cal looked around the room. "I know these are not the ideal circumstances, but I know you, and you love a challenge. Take your turn, Son."

Chase nodded. He couldn't believe Kate wouldn't tell him about the new job. No wonder she had been so reticent to talk about staying, or her feelings. He put his hand to his chest. He believed Kate might love him back, but he would deal with that later. Right now, he had a company to save. He stood and addressed the room. "Alright, everyone. I think we have some papers to sign. Let's do this."

Chapter 29: Kate

As the Governor's helicopter landed on the battered roof of KinCo, Kate finished reviewing the file Lindsey had sent her. She shut the laptop with a tiny click and a prayer she was not wrong about all of this. Before the blades could come to a stop, Kate jumped out of the copter, and bending down, ran towards the door.

She bolted up to the conference room and burst through the door just as Chase's hand was poised over a document. "Stop!" she yelled.

Chase looked up at her, and she could see relief and confusion flood his face. "Kate?" he asked in disbelief. "What are you doing here?"

Kate put her hand to her chest and struggled to catch her breath. "You can't sign those papers," she gasped.

Chase looked down at the papers and back to her, a deep line creasing his brow.

Donna Ogrodnick popped up in the corner. "Really, Peggy," she said, "you're going to let this girl run rough-shod over your meeting?"

Peggy lurched forward. "What are you doing, Kate?" She hissed. "Get out of here."

"Now hold on a minute," said Rose. "I'd like to hear what Kate has to say."

Kate put her laptop down on the conference table and took a breath. She looked at Chase. Their eyes locked, and she knew she was doing the right thing. "I need to speak to the family privately," she said.

Kenji Kai stood and straightened his suit. "This is very unorthodox," he said. "This is giving me too many pause. I think sign now or we leave."

Peggy put her hands on the table. "For Christ's sake, Chase, sign the papers."

Chase searched Kate's eyes and Kate felt a string form between them. "What is it, Kate? Just say it."

Kate took a deep breath. It was all or nothing. "I don't believe that this IPO is going forward in good faith," she said. "I believe Kenji Kai is planning to take over the company so he can steal the KinCo brand name and move the manufacturing to Asia."

Cal and Rose both stood in unison. "What?"

Cal bellowed. "Kai—is this true?"

"That's character assassination, Kate." Donna said from the other side of the table. "Even you know better than that. You must have proof to make an accusation like that. Do you?" Donna asked. "Do you have proof, Kate?"

Kate glared back at Donna. "I think the facts speak for themselves," Kate said. "A strange rash of PR nightmares seems to suddenly befall this company after decades of absolutely nothing. I thought that was strange, but if somebody was trying to tank the launch, they would have hit harder. Then I realized that wasn't the goal. You wanted the launch to happen, then you were going to set all of these PR blunders you've created ablaze and crater the stock price post-launch. The family would see all their assets and life work crumble right before their eyes. For Kai to get controlling interest of the company, you would only need to convince one family member to sell before it was too late."

"Don't be ridiculous, Kate," Cal said. "That can't be true. Nobody here would ever sell their stake in the company." Kate watched as Rose reached out her hand and put it on Cal's arm. Cal looked down, then dropped his head. When he raised it again, he looked over at Peggy.

Peggy sat in the corner, her face alight with anxiety. Her eyes darted from Chase to Cal then settled on Donna Ogrodnick. "Donna, are you setting me up?" Anger and hurt lined her face. "You were setting me up this whole time?"

"Don't be silly," said Donna. "These are all lies. I told you Kate Piper was a train-wreck. I told you she would come into your company, ingratiate herself with the men," she said, sneering at Chase, "and then destroy everything. That's what she does."

Chase turned to Donna. "Shut up, Ogrodnick. Kate's worth ten of you."

Several voices started talking at once; Rose was admonishing Peggy, Cal was speaking to Chase, and Kai's whole team began whispering. Kai stood and buttoned his jacket. "Enough!" he bellowed.

Everyone in the room turned and looked at him. "So, here we are," he said. "No difference. Same plan." He turned to Chase. "You sign the papers."

"The hell I will," said Chase.

"You will sign," Kai said, "or we will destroy your reputation. Your brand will crumble. You think all we have is a couple photos? A tweet?" he laughed. "No, if you don't sign, we go ahead, anyway. We will release everything. You will not recover."

"That's not true," said Kate. "I have a plan."

The conference room doors swung open and in walked the Governor. "Am I too late to the party?" he asked, turning to Kate.

"Just in time, Sir." Kate turned toward Chase and the rest of the family. "I explained to the Governor that if Kai and Ogrodnick succeeded, lots of Oklahoma jobs would be lost. So he has graciously agreed to co-sponsor a rebuilding initiative. He will put emphasis on rebuilding the roads around KinCo first, if KinCo agrees to keep jobs alive in Oklahoma." She watched as the Governor nodded his assent. "Also, to combat whatever ineffectual propaganda Ogrodnick unleashes, I suggest we move aggressively to the public with the following message." Kate propped up her laptop and pulled up a video. "Forgive the quality, it's a rough draft I did on the way here. Of course, my voice will be replaced by a professional."

The family turned to see the screen. A video began with a picture of the KinCo headquarters and Kate's narrative. "KinCo, an American Company for four generations. We believe in Oklahoma, we believe in America." Then the video ran through pictures of the original Kincaid Mill, the first general store, Rose in her lab coat holding a beaker. Then she and Cal holding a baby. The photos showed black and white images of Peggy as a young woman racing her horse, and Chase racing his car, then his crash, and photos of the company picnics, and Chase busting down doors to help his neighbors after the tornado. The voice over continued, "KinCo believes in

America, and they believe in their neighbors. We are committed to rebuilding after this storm, and are partnering with the Governor's office to keep Oklahoma and America strong."

Kate turned off the laptop and turned to the family. Rose, Cal, and Peggy sat together with their arms linked. Peggy's eyes flooded with tears.

Kate turned to Chase. He came around the table and threw his arms around her. "Kate," he said into her ear, then kissed her several times on the cheek. "You saved us. You saved me."

Kate shook her head. "No, you saved me. I never—" she sniffed, looking around. "Can we speak privately?"

"Clear the room," Chase said loudly.

Cal stood and grabbed the contracts, ripping them in shreds. "That means you, Kai. Get the hell out of here."

Kai uncrossed his arms and waved his hand for his team to follow him out the door. "You will regret this," he said as he walked out.

Peggy turned to Donna with her fists on her hips. "You really had me going, lady," she said. "Now, get your skinny ass out of our building before I carry it out."

Donna scurried after Kai and his team, then Cal, Rose, and Peggy walked out, patting each other on the back.

Chase and Kate watched the door shut, then

turned towards each other. Chase curled his hands through Kate's hair, then around her neck and lowered his lips to hers. Kate could feel the love in that kiss and melted into it.

"Chase, I was wrong. I'm sorry it took me so long. I love you," she said, wrapping her arms tightly around his waist. "I love you, and I don't know what that means for me, or for my life, I just know I do." She felt her body finally relax, and a happiness flood through her body she had never felt before.

Chase held her face in his hands and kissed her gently on the lips. "Kate," he said. "I'm all yours."

Epilogue

Kate kissed Chase and watched him saunter out to his truck. His jeans hugged the back of his legs in just the right way. God, that man was good looking. She touched her lips, feeling the warm buzz lingering on them. It was the same feeling she got every time she kissed him.

She turned to her computer and hit video call.

"Pipes!" Lindsey said, as she illuminated the screen. "How are you?"

Kate beamed into the camera. She could feel herself glowing. "Never better," she said. "I'm happy. Really, really happy."

"Aw, domestic bliss. Sounds nice." Lindsey smiled.

"It is," Kate said. "I can't believe I get to come home to a man I love every night."

"I'm so happy for you."

"Lindsey, listen. I have an offer for you."

Lindsey's brow shot up. "Do tell…"

"The rebuild on my old bungalow is almost done. Chase and I would like to offer it to you. We'd like you to move out here to Oklahoma."

"Pipes, I…"

"Now, hold on. I know you are a Boston girl, but I think you'll really love it as much as I do. The people are amazing, and all our Boston clients have agreed to this being our home-base. What do you think?"

Lindsey sighed then tipped her head. "Pipes, I really appreciate the offer, I do. But…there's something I need to tell you."

"Okay…"

"Well, you really inspired me, you know, going after your dreams. And I decided it's time for me to do the same. Can't be a basement dork forever, you know. It's time for me to get out of my mom's house. So…I'm going to college." Lindsey finished with a smile.

"College!"

"Yeah, I know I'm a little older than most of the students will be, but they are giving me a pass on my first two years of credits because of my mad skills. And, get this, I get to work with some of the best technical minds in the country. They want me to work with some special, undercover data research team. The details are fuzzy, but I'm psyched."

Kate paused for a beat, then said, "College. Wow, Lindz. I couldn't be happier for you."

"Really?"

"Yeah. I hope they know how lucky they are to have you."

"Thanks, Pipes. You know, we'll be friends forever, and I'll always jump in when you need me."

"I know, but don't you worry about me. You go get your degree, and whatever comes after that. You are Lindsey Monahan, and they don't know who they're messing with, right?"

Lindsey felt passion spring in her gut. She was going to have her own adventure. "Right!"

Please read on to get a small taste of the hot, tumultuous adventure Lindsey finds herself in! If you've enjoyed *Chasing Kate*, please leave a review on the site from which you purchased it. Reviews are the lifeblood of all authors, and I'm no exception! Thank you!

Chapter Excerpt From

Loving Lindsey

An American Dream Love Story ~ Book Two

Lindsey trailed soft, light kisses up his torso and onto his open mouth. "What?" She teased as she stood on her toes, wrapping her arms around his neck. "You don't want me to leave?" Before he could answer, she slid her tongue just inside his lips. His arms tensed, and with two giant hands, he swung her around so he pressed against her from behind, the soft palm of his right hand pulling her back against him. A spark ignited within her as his lips began to caress the back of her neck.

"You can't leave," he murmured against the back of her ear. "Not when things are just getting interesting."

Lindsey felt herself fill with a pleasant, wanting liquid. "No," she sputtered, warmth filling her spine. "I'm not moving out. I'm just moving in."

He spun her back around, his beautiful face glowing at her words. He deftly swept her up into his arms and carried her to the sofa. He laid her down then straightened. His desire filled gaze slowly trailed from her mouth to her breasts, then to the lace panties that clung lightly to her shapely hips. She wondered if he could sense how wet she was. She hoped that he could.

He lunged forward, laying the perfect length of his body against hers, his body so warm and solid that her legs spread instinctively beneath him, allowing him to sink even closer.

Her muscles tensed and swelled in anticipation. *Maybe this day wasn't a total bust after all,* she thought absently. Of all the things she had longed to experience in her life, a hook-up with a beautiful stranger wasn't on the list. But now, cradled in this man's arms, his lips and groin pressing against her, she decided this was one experience she was looking forward to having. She heard these one night stands went from hot to awkward fast, but the way he touched her felt like...well, like love. Maybe she was crazy, but she allowed herself to sink into the moment, the dream of her new life expanding quite nicely.

She took his beautiful face in both of her hands and pulled away to look into his light eyes. They were filled with anticipation and longing, but with none of the doubt she would have expected from a man she'd just met. She caressed the strong, golden line of his jaw and smiled. He smiled back and took her hand, kissing the palm as he stared into her eyes, then massaged her breast lightly as he planted tiny kisses all around her nipple, effectively sending tingling desire shooting through her body. As he trailed his fingertips down the curve of her belly and beneath her panties, he stroked the moist hair between her legs. She sighed and trembled.

"I could do this all day," he said.

"Okay," Lindsey whispered, her voice begging. In response, his hand slid across her in a slick, rapid motion. She felt herself swell at the thought that he would soon be deep inside of her. She felt his body tense as well, and thought he must be thinking the same thing until his hand slowed to a stop. He went suddenly still and she realized his eyes were wide as he stared at something across the room. She craned her head to see what he was looking at. She looked across the boxes to the bank of monitors and CPUs she had arranged on the kitchen counter. She felt his body go stiff.

"What?" she asked. "What is it?"

He jumped up from the sofa in a shot and began to look around. He turned in circles, his eyes wide.

Lindsey got up onto her knees, pulling a pillow across her naked chest. "You're freaking me out," she whispered.

She watched as he charged across the room to the kitchen where her moving receipt still lay on the counter, alarmed at the sight of every muscle in his beautiful body tightening.

He turned toward her, the paper crumpled into his fist. "What the hell is this?"

"Um, my moving receipt. Why?"

He took several long breaths, then glared at her,

accusation etched on his face. His muscles tensed before speaking. "You're good," he said, shaking his head as he reached out and snatched up his scattered clothes. "You almost had me."

Lindsey's mouth went slack. "What?"

He turned toward her, his eyes flashing. "You hacked me! And I actually thought that—that...never mind," he said, shoving his legs into his pants.

Lindsey felt her mouth go dry. "What?" she asked. "I…What?"

"I'm so stupid," he spat, shaking his head. "Of course you did." He grabbed his shirt and shoes, his face growing red. "You found out where I lived, moved in, then—" His palm slid over his face in one slow, regretful motion. "You seduced me." He swung toward her. "Right? *Right!?* Admit it."

"I— "

"Don't deny it," he said. "You hackers and your stupid games. But you," he continued, now pointing at her, "you viper, you take things to a whole new level, right? It's not enough to hack me. You had to screw with my head too."

Lindsey felt a trickle of light begin to seep into her brain. How could he know her moniker was Viper? *Only*—oh no. "Wait," she began, her voice trembling. "You can't be…you're..." She could barely get the words out. "Professor Wheeler?"

He stood and looked at her flatly, the veins in his arms and neck bulging.

"Hah," he spat. "Like you didn't know that. You

waited at that bar. You brought me here!"

"Hold on a minute," Lindsey said, standing with the pillow still clutched to her chest. "You brought *me* here, not the other way around."

"Nice try," he said. "Like we just happened to live in the same building."

Lindsey tried to calm her heart rate. She felt her whole life begin to swirl down a dark and irreversible drain as she spoke. "Campus housing put me here," she said slowly. "They said the dorms were full, they—"

"Save it," Zach said as he tugged open her front door. "You're out. Don't you step a foot near my lab."

The door slammed with a bang and Lindsey fell back onto the sofa, listening to Zach's heavy footsteps storm down the stairwell. A moment later, she heard the door to the unit just below hers open and slam fatally shut.

Tears sprung to her eyes. How had this happened? She hadn't even started the program and it was over? Her mind spun through his words over and over until their finality truly sank in. Her dream was over. She curled up around her pillow and sobbed.

She should have just stayed in her mom's basement, safe in her virtual world. Isn't that where she had always belonged anyway?

About the Author

Josephine Parker has been writing, reading, and loving books for 30 years. She holds a fine-arts degree in Creative Writing from the University of Colorado-Boulder, and has worked as a literary agent, freelance writer, and editor before embarking on her own dream of owning several small businesses and writing books. She splits her time between Denver and Seattle with the love of her life and their very needy cat.

Josephine followed her own American Dream, and now invites readers to join her heroines in fulfilling their dreams and finding true love.

She also loves to interact with readers. You can find her on twitter @JosiePBooks, facebook.com/josiepbooks or keep up to date on new releases, free short stories, and her newsletter by going to her website at jp-books.com.

She is available for interviews, podcasts, and book clubs.

Made in the USA
Columbia, SC
10 November 2018